MIRUNA, A TALE

BOGDAN SUCEAVĂ

MIRUNA, A TALE

TRANSLATED FROM THE ROMANIAN
BY ALISTAIR IAN BLYTH

TWISTED SPOON PRESS
PRAGUE
2014

ISBN 978-80-86264-44-8

Published with the kind support of the Translation and
Publication Support Program of the Romanian Cultural
Institute, Bucharest.

INSTITUTUL
CULTURAL
R O M Â N

CONTENTS

1

I remember my first school holiday. Our parents took us to spend two weeks in Evil Vale, but Miruna, my sister, didn't want to go because Mother had told her Grandfather was a giant. "I don't like you playing tricks on me," Miruna told her. "Giants are in fairy tales. Grandpa is just a normal man." But I saw the way she eyed him when he came out to greet us. There was some truth in what Mother had told us: the stature of the giant from long ago remained, only now he moved laboriously, barely able to walk. His back was rigid, as though something in it had snapped, and it could no longer swivel this way or that, and I heard Mother telling our father that he had problems urinating — I remember being surprised. What she said annoyed me. Should such things really be discussed? I cannot claim to have understood the situation very well. Now, after so many years, I realize that back then I comprehended nothing at all. I looked at Grandfather and knew nothing about his illness, or where he came from, or the story of his life, and I wasn't really prepared to find out. At the time I had read no more than a volume of *Undying Tales*, and I had seen a serial on television about the African jungle called *Daktari* and also the show about Flipper, the dolphin. *The Goat and Her Three Kids* bored me and *Cinderella* irritated me, although the cartoon version seemed to be Miruna's favorite. I preferred *Tom and Jerry*, and couldn't wait to watch it on TV every Sunday afternoon at two. I noticed Grandfather wasn't interested in television, and he didn't listen to the radio and completely ignored music. I saw that his clothes were unlike any I'd ever seen anyone wearing in Pitești or anywhere else, and to me he looked good in white. He wore a white shirt stitched with red and black wavy lines that descended to below his girdle, and his coarse white trousers looked clean to me as if by a miracle, because I'd always get dirty when I played, and Miruna even more so, because she was a tomboy. Many years later, when Miruna and I recalled those days, she told me she now realized we'd had a grandfather whose likeness could have been exhibited in a museum, like the kind found in dioramas, as if a member of a lost tribe or an exotic people. While he was alive, no one would have dared to think anything like that, because he had a voice like thunder and eyes that blazed, and every so often he would curse so fiercely that little tornadoes would whirl the object of his curse up into the air and cast him ten paces yonder.

When we arrived in Evil Vale that summer, Grandfather showed us the only sign of weakness he ever allowed himself. He told me I was his grandson with the name of an emperor, Trajan, and when he took me in his arms, I felt his rough cheek. As he was hugging me, Grandmother asked Mother how many days she would be leaving us there. Neither I nor Miruna cried, I mean, we didn't cry then, straightaway, but much later, in the evening, or maybe it was at midnight, like two abandoned, pathetic children who were already in the habit of laughing or crying in unison, always for reasons adults could not understand. Even at that age we were both a bit odd. Miruna would smile even if she were sad. She later picked up Grandmother's habit of mending all things with a needle and thread, much like the way Cousin Matei would get the urge to hammer nails into any wooden object he found. Cousin Matei was already attending school, but we weren't. That was the summer he received a hiding for having tried to saw through the wooden well bucket, and water leaked over his father's trousers.

In the evenings, Grandfather would sit on the porch of the wooden house he had built at the end of the sixties, leaving the big house to his children so that their affairs wouldn't get mixed up in any way, although he and Grandmother continued to share the same farmyard with Matei and his folks. But Grandfather was different from the others. The evening after our parents departed and for the first time we were left in our grandmother's care, I heard him telling Miruna that this was the only place where you could see time passing, where it was never entirely frozen. I was in a spot of the garden where along two furrows at the edge of a row of plum trees the tips of freshly planted blades of wheat sprouted from the earth. Miruna didn't understand what he said. I didn't understand anything either. She asked where you could see time passing, and Grandfather told her about the enchantments of each grain of wheat, where the image of Our Lord Jesus Christ is secretly graven. Once sown in the earth, the new grains bear the mystery of the resurrection, and this is why the wheat sprouts, because of that image engraved on each grain.

"Where is it?" Miruna asked again, looking between the two furrows for the grain of wheat graven with the image.

Grandfather looked at us as though he was about to burst out laughing. Was he testing us? Perhaps. Did he want to see how much we believed or how much we understood of what he was telling us? As it was, neither one of us still believed in Father Christmas or other fairy tales. But then Grandfather grew serious once more. It's possible that in the telling he began to relive all those events, the visible mingling with the invisible, the childish with the adult, the what-should-not-be-uttered with silence, the past with the never happened. He told us so many things we did not understand at the time. It was only much later, when we remembered them, did they begin to coalesce. He was to place before us on a stage tales that might have seemed unsuited to our age, and he put such passion into the telling you would've thought he were reliving everything from the very beginning for our sake alone. It all sounded very different to Miruna. She was much younger than I, and she had inherited his vision as well, such that an entire world passed into her, and she became heir to a separate realm, the memory of which is with her today. The tales became real in her mind, and our grandfather, Niculae Berca, found it necessary in the two summers that followed to measure out the stories in doses, or to alter the ones she already knew and augment them to reflect her age. One tale arose from another, multiplying and growing more complex, so that every day Miruna was plunged into a marvelous ocean. Those wonders really did exist for her, the most magical apparitions taking on a material body. Miruna eventually came to conceive the world in the form of a fairy tale, living for years in a world full of the fantastical, which gave her the air of being a child prodigy, one of those who know something of history and geography before they even start attending school but who cannot say for sure if King Carol and Prâslea the Brave lived at the same time or if one came before the other. In the world of fairy tales, everything is muddled, and time most of all, so in Miruna's mind's eye she was actually witnessing the battles fought by Stephen the Great along with the exploits of the brave Greuceanu and the song of the silver bird — they were all superimposed on the same background and all mixed in with the wise sayings of Anton Pann from the book that Grandfather kept at the head of his bed, under the quilt, or the *Romance of Alexander* from which he read us the story of the magnificent war Alexander the Great waged against the birds and butterflies in the Land of Indus, which lies much farther away than the wood of magical beasts guarding the palace of ageless youth and immortal life. Did we believe these stories were true? For a time we naturally believed everything. For Miruna, this *was* the world. Those stories concealed disquietudes within that would later be revealed. Today, I don't know if Grandfather realized what consequences his stories would have, but he once told us something, as if he were speaking to adults, that only now I understand: a well-tempered blend of tales carries the entire world on its back and ultimately explains the world to us from inside out. Were it not for those tales to remind us just how things stood, then May-the-Bells-Slay-Him, the black devil in the mural of the Last Judgment on the church porch who lurks at the bottom of the wall to the right of the door and who frightened Miruna whenever she passed, would throw the world out of kilter to then set it to another law, according to his mind and his reckoning. When Grandfather took us to church, Miruna would hide behind him from the image of the devil painted by the bottom of the door.

"Does he exist, Grandpa?"

He shrugged and said no more, which did not at all reassure Miruna. I heard Grandfather telling Mother to let the children be raised in Evil Vale, at least for a time, as it would be the right thing to do, necessary, in his mind, and our parents told him it would be better if he minded his own health. How's that, mind his own health? His mind was to talk to us as often as he could. Grandmother thought she knew everything there was to know about her husband, and nothing out of the blue could just change him. She knew how cantankerous he could be, as if he were always dissatisfied with folks and with what he saw around him. This is why, thinking of their eight children and eleven grandchildren, she told him:

"It's the first time you've taken interest in a child since you taught Maria carols."

Maria was our mother, though even she hadn't inherited Grandfather's blue eyes, or his way of telling or listening to a tale. It seems this connection had been established only with Miruna, for I am not like her, and the tale I am telling here is not even half of what either of them would have been able to tell, had they ever had a mind to do so. When Grandfather told a tale, events seemed to cohere all by themselves, and he seemed to rise above the story, gazing down on it from great heights, and, his gaze having taken it in, he would lay out the episodes and all the details in an order that left you breathless, like a hawk swooping down from high above.

Every afternoon, or so it seemed to me, Grandfather would be waiting on his bench by the gate for the sun to set. Sunset in the valleys between the mountains always takes place earlier. All three of us would go to wait for the newspaper. He would sit on the bench by the gate, wearing one of his white shirts, his black hat perched on his head, a Gypsy king having strayed far from his imaginary kingdom. When it was cool, he would sometimes wear his waistcoat with the four large buttons — Miruna used to call them the four moons on Grandpa — from which hung the chain of his Roskopf Patent 1918 pocket watch that I wanted to play with but wasn't allowed. The watch came into my hands later, because in the complicated divvying up of the family possessions I inherited it. Twilight was the hour when a red sickle sliced the clouds with flaming tongues, and Grandfather would fall silent and his tales momentarily break off. The postman was an elderly fellow, but not as elderly as Grandfather, who rose from his stool or bench when he saw him coming, and they would exchange greetings and small talk for a moment about what was going on, always about people we didn't know and about whom we'd never heard.

"We were in the war together," Grandfather told us once, pointing to the postman.

We understood their complicity in the battle with time old men always feel alone in waging. Grandfather would take the newly arrived copy of *The Spark* in his left hand and, his fingers blackened by the newsprint, take a few steps holding the folded paper, then open it before settling back down on the bench. He would look at the daily photograph on the front page of Nicolae Ceaușescu at a meeting of the Central Committee or at some parade, or receiving letters of accreditation from a new African ambassador or at a plenary session, and he would read the caption to the photograph aloud, pulling out his pocket watch and looking at the time, all of which seemed to Miruna a furtive sign that Grandfather understood that all the tales the newspaper told had taken place long ago. The arrival of the newspaper seemed to break the mechanism that was Grandfather, which was set to function perfectly only in its own, separate time, without interference from the distant world. In fact, only now have I come to realize that as Niculae Berca looked at the front page of a newspaper not even a quarter as interesting as the gazettes of old, he would remember a host of achievements and exploits entangled with those dead in the war and of premature aging, stories of loves as ancient as the world and of the wrack and ruin of long faded endeavors, the sorts of things he wouldn't have told us children for anything in the world, the sum of which in his mind had secretly contributed to the present state of affairs. We were too young for him to tell us everything, but his curiosity in how some present-day story might ultimately develop had to come from somewhere, such as the story of the Vietnam War, or the investigations into the Palestinian terrorists at the Munich Olympics, or the launch of the latest Sputnik, or a coup in this or that Central American country. He would turn the newspaper from first page to last, to read about the story of the present, in which time could be felt struggling in its womb. And this would stir other tales into existence, and time would quickly turn back to days that Miruna and I, Trajan, could see with his eyes, exchanging places with him, as he began to tell a fantastic tale that occurred when he was our age. I had only just learned to read. It was before the First World War, when Father's eyesight was failing. Then he saw his father, Constantine Berca, paying the first newspaper subscription ever to be taken in Evil Vale, a newspaper that would makes its way to him in the Făgăraș Mountains with a delay of two days after its print date, because that was how long it took the post from Bucharest to arrive in those days.

"You'll be the one who'll read it most," Constantine Berca told him, rubbing his eyes.

Niculae had a hard time reading back then, building up each word letter by letter, intoning them as though they were complicated tales, which on his lips always acquired a whiff of the unreal. Even so, he comprehended nothing of what he read. He was incapable of imagining the king. He could not imagine any Royal Palace. Yet it might have been *The Universe* daily rather than a primer that taught him sooner that year how to syllabize, slowly and smoothly, with limpid diction and relaxed lips. The mail, newspaper and all, would arrive at dusk. That it reached Evil Vale was the greatest miracle of the modern world, a link with the whole planet via the written and printed word. His hands were small and white, and the ink rubbed off onto his fingertips just as it does today. But this was something entirely different: it was the news. They would all gather in the big room while Niculae's sister, Mara, sewed by the light of the same gas lamp he used to read the newspaper. Sitting there with him were his older brothers, Gheorghe and Ioan, who then went off to war in Bulgaria along with the entire Muscel Regiment, never to return, and their father, Constantine Berca, no older than fifty at the time. The Great War had not yet taken place, nor had the war against the Bulgarians; the world was a more peaceful place and misfortune was not yet filling the news as it would in the 1930s when lawless deeds were threaded one after another like beads and the newspapers had no greater joy than to tell the tale of one calamity after another. On that evening, for example, the gigantic headline EXPLOSION AT PUCIOASA introduced one of the events that terrified people at the beginning of the 20th century — Niculae read the story seated on a box of wool combs and sewing needles: "At Mr. Longin Dobrescu's mill in Pucioasa a worker's carelessness has resulted in a terrible accident. Mrs. Dobrescu has a brandy distiller at the mill. Gheorghe Elena Lopătaru, the worker in question, placed a canister of gasoline next to the still to heat it up. The heated gasoline exploded, leaving Lopătaru with severe burns on his face and hands, and another five workers with burns less severe. The imprudent worker was admitted to Târgoviște Hospital in critical condition, while the other five workers received treatment from Dr. Petre Dumitrescu in Pucioasa."

"What's the point of writing about this in the newspaper?" asked Mara.

"But wasn't the mill damaged?" asked Gheorghe.

"Of course it was damaged," their father explained, "after all, everyone inside ended up with burns."

"Was Gheorghe older than you, Grandpa?" Miruna interrupted the story.

"Five years older, just as Trajan is one year older than you," answered Grandfather, showing Miruna how to count with her fingers.

"But it doesn't say anywhere that the explosion was inside," Gheorghe said, analyzing every word. "Maybe the brandy still was outside."

"Why do I have only one brother, Grandpa?" asked Miruna, looking at me.

Grandfather shrugged and avoided the question.

Two days after reading the first news, Niculae Berca — recalling the story of almost seventy years ago as if it were yesterday — read to them again by the light of the lamp, from the

"Miscellaneous" section: "Worker Gheorghe Elena Lopătaru, victim of the unfortunate accident a few days ago, died yesterday at Târgoviște Hospital. His death was caused by the wounds suffered from . . ."

"Why have you stopped, Niculae? Carry on," said Gheorghe.

The boy stood holding the newspaper like a shield, leaning into the lamplight.

"No, don't read it," his father told him, placatingly, his thoughts remote, rolling himself a cigarette. Then Niculae looked at another page and read something else, the story of death still before his eyes. All these things were linked by the word. For every story in the newspaper, somewhere far away someone was sad or happy, someone died or brought children into the world. All were linked. After reading such a sad story, Niculae's voice became toneless, and his impassive reading no longer had his parents and brothers listening to him as if he were a prophet from distant lands. With every newspaper he read, the misfortunes seemed to grow ever larger, much larger than the first he had read. With endings ever more deplorable, the calamities becoming increasingly unavoidable, as though everyone and everything were hurtling toward a pit full of gunpowder: "On a level crossing near Bordeaux, a train collided with an automobile containing four people. Three persons were killed and another five seriously injured."

"Enough," said Constantine Berca, "I don't want to hear about any more disasters. Only bad things happen these days."

Niculae would then turn the newspaper over and peruse the classifieds offering items for sale, the more reassuring ones, the ones reasonably priced, the ones never causing heart pangs. Constantine Berca wanted to find out about distant events, but what he heard and saw was completely different than what he would have wished to hear. Even for a man who had been to war.

Constantine Berca, our great-grandfather, also used to tell stories from long ago, and for a time neither Miruna nor I knew which of these stories were his and which were Grandfather's. Everything was so mixed up together that we could not tell anything apart. Yet I now see them in a different light, and I am the one writing them here. After having given voice to the stories in the newspaper, Niculae for the first time began to think that some of them were just plain lies. His months of reading had left his mind with a growing suspicion that newspapers are a muddle that mingle truth with rumor, such as the stories concocted by old women in villages with nothing better to do, all kinds of startling goings-on that in time prove to be lies. Such a news story would leave his father muttering something like: "That's something Old Woman Fira could've cooked up." Thus Niculae discovered that when you read news about an unfortunate event it's possible to care about a person you've never seen, some person faraway, as much as you care about yourself. He no longer even knew who'd told him this. But the point was that in his mind their link to the world was via a page in a newspaper where fabrications could creep in, and this is what left people dumbfounded. He began to measure the evenings in lies and truths, in half-truths, because this is what filled the newspapers. His reading of the news gave him the impression that people lived in the constant fear that evil happening elsewhere might befall them. Is that all there is to it, is this why we wait for the newspaper to arrive with the mail from Bucharest? Is this why such news stories link us to the world? On one such evening, Niculae heard for the first time one of those stories that are not meant to answer anything in particular but still have something to say about what's going in the world. It was one of the stories his father used to tell about the Battle of Rahova, during the Romanian War of Independence in 1877–78. This happened when Constantine Berca was very young, for he was very young when he went off to war.

Before the war, Constantine had a good friend in Evil Vale named Gheorghe Negru. They were both in the same company and they both fought in the same battles, but only one returned. They were still at the front when they found out that each soldier was going to be given a plot of land. The rumor reached them after the battles had ended and the Turks had been rounded up into sad convoys of prisoners marching toward the Danube under the escort of the cavalry corps. The newspaper claimed that the government would give them land upon their return home. But as it happened, they were shunted here and there with paperwork until October, when it was determined which plot of land from the old monastic estates each would receive. This mountain had once belonged to the Argeș Monastery. And before that, long before that, the mountain had belonged to another, distant monastery on Mount Athos, whose name no one now recalls. After the war these lands were apportioned. Niculae Berca heard from his father the story of the war against the Turks, of the assault on the fortifications of Rahova, of the exploits of Circassian and Cossack horsemen, of the Russian officers' samovar for brewing tea on the front line, which was not dented even when hit by bullets, of the colonel who drank so much vodka before a battle that his guts caught fire when the Turks shot him and he blazed like a matchstick, of the stray bullet at the end of the battle that ripped the pip off soldier Constantine Berca's left epaulette on the Sunday of St. Peter, at lunchtime, of all those trials of life and, above all, of death under the appellation of war. Having survived the stray bullet, Berca decided he had been spared only because he still had something to achieve in this world. All these events seemed to him connected, they had a purpose within some longer and larger occurrence we shall never glimpse in its entirety.

"It's damned good to find out, the lots having been drawn, that I'm not going to croak in this war."

This thought, it is said, came to him at the bottom of a shell crater among corpses with distant faces. The battle left Berca with a game left leg, and for the rest of his life he limped. Niculae found out from his father's stories how only a few weeks after the fall of the redoubt, after the Muscel Regiment's glorious, victorious assault, in which two thirds of the soldiers had remained behind to fertilize those fields, when the fighting continued all along the line from the Danube to the Balkan Mountains, a number of badly depleted companies had received the order to bring back to Romania some wretched Turks who had been taken prisoner. It was with such a convoy that they returned, wounded, homeward. While they were still in the Turkish part of the world, soldier Constantine Berca had laid down his rifle and his knapsack, and he made a hole in a cartridge to extract the gunpowder. And when they reached the bridgehead over the Danube, he sprinkled the powder on the water and gazed at it to see what tomorrow would bring, to read the future in it. The one who saw him do this, they say, was a lieutenant by the name of Todiraş Rădulescu, who came up to him, his shoulder bandaged beneath his cape, for he, too, had been wounded in Bulgaria, and asked him what he was doing there, leaning over the bridge. Constantine Berca gazed at the Danube and said he had to see if there was any truth in the belief that if you cast a swallow on flowing water and it floats upstream against the current, it is a sign of death, that is, going against the flow is a sign of death written on the water. The lieutenant looked him up and down and recognized his ailment. He touched him and noticed he had a fever; he was burning like the hob of a stove. He called the medics and informed them that the soldier was delirious.

Constantine Berca languished for a month and a half in the hospital, and when he was discharged he was unrecognizable: he was so thin his skin had acquired the transparency only the bones lying hidden beneath the skin possess, the very state saints are said to achieve through unceasing prayer and life beyond death. He looked as though he had crossed over the water at the ends of the earth and then back again. But he was whole; he had not lost his leg.

Then came demobilization, and he returned to Evil Vale. In autumn, he went to Câmpulung, where they were handing out the deeds for land to the veterans of the Muscel Regiment. There had been no news of Gheorghe Negru, about where he had vanished after the battle, or whether he was alive or dead. He was said to have wandered off in the thick of battle, but his folks were still waiting for him at home, and fortunetelling and spells told that he was still alive. Constantine Berca received a property deed at the autumn hour of mellowed fruit, when laws were being established under new signs, like a last-minute erratum to books as old as the world. For us, Berca's people, it was as though history began right then and there, because no one in the family had ever owned land before that. Before, there had only been the mountain, naked, bare, with its wildernesses and mists that on autumn mornings buried Evil Vale and Red Cliff and the Knoll.

At first, the land to be parceled out after the war was nothing but a mass of words on paper. They say it took the officials in Câmpulung two days to work out which piece of land went to which soldier. Before the war, Constantine Berca had been a serving boy at an inn, and the down had barely begun to sprout on his chin when he had volunteered to go to war. Now tall and thin, he had returned home with that piece of paper. He received land on Old Knoll, a gigantic squashed sphere of a hill on the way to the village of Ne'er-Do-Well. He had never seen the land there, and did not yet know what rockiness and wildness surrounded it. It was the only sandy hill among so many green hills of good loam. When he found himself with the papers in his hand, he carefully stowed them in his broad waistband alongside his veteran's service record. On that day, he bought from a German's shop in Câmpulung, as though it were the thing of wonder that it was, a Swiss pendulum clock with a crystalline chime, a white, nacreous face, Roman numerals, and gold-colored weights, which he intended to put in the new house he intended to build with his own hands. He brought back the pendulum clock in the cart of a forester from Domnești, on a Monday, at the beginning of a sunny week in autumn. He stayed for a while in a ramshackle wooden hovel broken by time and oblivion with weeds and thistles growing everywhere, in which no one had lived for more than twenty years. The farmyard was overrun by thistles, like a plague. The beams were damp, moldering, and riddled with woodworm, and the shutters rattled when the wind blew. The whitewash had peeled like leprous skin, revealing the loam that glued together the woodwork. At night, in the old wooden bed, he would hear the woodworms working so industriously that it would wake him. A lame badger had set up home in the chimney. Constantine Berca took the pendulum clock home and set it according to his own reckoning, after looking at the position of the sun, for there was no other clock in Evil Vale, nor had there ever been. He hung it on the east wall, next to the old wooden icon depicting the Mother of God weeping for the crucified Christ that had been part of his mother's dowry when she arrived from Transylvania. He listened for a few moments to the ticking of the clock drowning out the gnawing of the woodworms, and then he paid the man with the cart after unloading all the things purchased in Câmpulung, things that now all had to be put in their proper places. This would take him much longer than he at first thought, and, as Grandfather told it to us, it was a task still unfinished. Constantine Berca cut the weeds, repaired the shutters and the door so that winter would not come on him under the open sky. He still had a fever when he met with the innkeeper, a man by the name of Constantine Dulubaș, we were told, a name that has come down to us, and this Dulubaș asked him what he had in mind now that he was back from the war. Constantine Berca told him he'd received some land, and he wanted to work it. But the innkeeper knew what kind of land it was, he knew its paltry value and how poor it was around Old Knoll. The place is a wilderness, trees need to be planted, you'll have to wait for the trees to bear fruit, the grass has to be rid of the weeds that overrun the meadows, this is what he likely told him. You'll need two or three years before you can make any money out of the place. Up there on the mountain, it takes years for things to fulfill their purpose. And he asked Berca if he wanted to come back to work at the inn. It was a good life, as he well knew, having grown up there. But Constantine Berca did not want to. He thanked the innkeeper for his concern and told him he wanted to manage on his own.

In those days, information about what folks did, what they said, and how they lived would be gleaned from the utterances of Old Woman Fira, who was to live for more than one hundred and fifty years, so long that even Miruna and I met her when we were little, Grandfather assuring us that she looked the same as she did when he was a child. She was the mouth of the village, she brought the news, she knew everything and passed it on. She had plenty to tell about Constantine Berca for a good few weeks, passing from one goodwife to another, from gate to gate, when the women would work of an evening and gossip among themselves. Old Woman Fira did not have a single tooth in her head, so that it was a wonder her cheeks still had form. It was probably around this time she stopped eating and lived on water alone. Her words could barely be understood, and sometimes, when her sight became troubled, she would mix Romanian and Serbian and no one could understand anything. Her eyes were usually half-closed and her back half-bent. Her homespun skirt would trail over the ground, and you would have said she was treading on air. One end of her girdle hung below her jerkin, ready to come undone. Such was the wraith that wended through the village while saying:

"Berca's lad has come into money, he's returned to the house of those old folk who died during the great plague in Prince Cuza's time, to the house whistling wind, instead of spending his money from the army wisely he bought a German's peerless pendulum clock, for a princely sum. Dulubaș, proud as he is, asked him to come back to work at the inn, for he's short of help, but that Berca lad would have none of it. He doesn't even have anything to eat. It'll be a wonder if he lasts the winter."

And Constantine Berca thought the same when he saw his land at Old Knoll for the first time. It was a few days before the first autumn rime, bad weather lurking in the skies, white puffy clouds like loaves of mist descending each morning to the earth or rising from the spines of the surrounding mountains, taking on shape. The journey to Old Knoll had taken him an hour. It was an out-of-the-way place where no one passed. The gigantic weeds rose as high as the trees and the knobbly bushes competed with the brambles for dry earth full of clods and stones.

"Was it long ago, Grandpa?" asked Miruna, interrupting the thread of the tale.

Grandfather reckoned it up in his mind and frowned like his father:

"A hundred years. But had it been a thousand the tale would be no different."

Toward the valley and to the right, toward the orchard of Enache Mâzgău, one saw a reddish, stony earth, a slope of the utmost poverty. Constantine Berca made the sign of the cross, spat in his palms, and scythed the thistles, and then he bore them home as though they were the richest hay. He made a cart to transport it to the hayrick a day before the frost of the first day of winter settled. One Sunday he came back from market with a cow and a bullock and some more hay for winter. No one understood how he was not mired in debt and how in just a few weeks he had put together a farm that would have taken others a lifetime. He sealed the cracks in the barn with clay until he was convinced the cold would be kept out. He replaced the windows and made new shutters. He fixed the gate to the road so that it opened and shut properly. He repaired the wicker fence around the yard. He patched up the roof until it managed to keep out the rain.

A harsh winter followed, one of those winters that consumes whole cartloads of wood in the stove, with cruel frosts, with snows that hid all the land and every last trace of the work of human hands, a winter that plunged the world back into its primordial state.

In Evil Vale, humans were not yet entirely master. There were only a handful of houses. In winter, wolf tracks dotted the snow in the village itself, wild boars rooted in the gardens not two paces away from folks, and lynxes prowled over the roofs. The villagers understood nature as hostile and inimical to them, and they did not rise up against it, for you would need to drink your brains away to rise against something so overwhelming. They all knew Evil Vale was a place in thrall to the forest, a place where human laws held no sway, where the laws of the wilderness governed. This lasted until the night when the entire village heard an unprecedented thunderclap that shook the earth and sky, and Old Woman Fira rushed the next morning to tell everyone just what had transpired:

"That madman Constantine Berca, after getting hay from dry earth and measuring time with a German's clock, now has a German rifle with two nostrils of flame, and it did to death a wolf last night."

In fact, a battle of life and death was being waged under the very eyes of the folks of Evil Vale. Night after night a thunderclap could be heard, each time Berca killed yet another wolf as soon as it had leapt his wicker fence. He could not frighten them with fire, or with noise, but in his yard he dealt out justice in the way he had learned on the battlefield at Rahova. At the bottom of the garden a huge tumulus appeared in which, in spite of the earth being frozen like a stone, he buried entire packs of wolves. A hill formed at the back of the house, and when Miruna was a child wolf skulls polished by time had been unearthed when they wanted to plant apple and pear trees there. So uncommon was Constantine Berca's zeal to establish order in his own homestead that Old Woman Fira could not stop herself from asking him one day, when she saw him doing chores around the woodpile in the yard, why he didn't drive away the wolves with torches and spells, as any other man would do, instead of angering the powers of the forest by lawlessly slaying them and in such great number. He replied that there is a time for building and a time for tearing down, and he told her many other things about foundations and purposes that Old Woman Fira could not grasp, because she could not understand what this man was saying, as though he were speaking an unknown language. Yet one year, on St. Venera's Day, in the middle of winter before Christmas, at the hour when bands of carolers were passing through the mist, Old Woman Fira told everyone up and down the village:

"Constantine Berca is a true beast. Wolves aren't the most savage on earth, he is."

Then the people of the village saw Constantine Berca as he was: not wholly God-fearing and religious, not wholly savage. He was half-man, half-beast, and this is what made them all think more carefully about their purpose in those mountains. From the child who had remained alone in the world never to know the age of fairy tales and wonders to the man who had gone to war, what the villagers saw was a transformation from that of imperfect angel into wolf. And something else was different about him, too. Constantine Berca worked at one thing at a time, and he did not go to the next task until he had finished the first. This was something new in Evil Vale, where as a rule tasks were jumbled together and nothing had either beginning or end.

Whenever she passed along the road in front of his house, Old Woman Fira would take care to cast a glance into the yard to see what cursed thing Berca was up to now. More often than not she would see him fixing immemorial objects for which no one else would have any use, chopping gnarled wood, striking with the sledgehammer when the axe remained stuck in a frozen log, or resting on his feet, with his game leg safely tucked to one side, the sign of a man who had lived through the ordeal of death and returned. One evening, Old Woman Fira saw him through the window kneeling by a candle, praying and making the sign of the cross like any other Christian. Then, when he blew on the flame to extinguish it, she saw how the light in his room slowly withdrew into the flame, gliding from the far corners of the room like a snake curling itself up in a box. The following Sunday, when Constantine Berca came to church to hear the liturgy, to pray together with all the villagers, to say the Lord's Prayer and the Creed, folks moved to one side, away from him, because the whole village had by now heard the rumor that he was no ordinary man, for in his house there was a candle whose light goes out in the opposite way to light in the rest of the world.

Berca's hunting of wolves and other wild beasts surpassed in its daring anything that had ever been seen or heard in Evil Vale, or even in the whole of the valley of Our Lady's River. And this was because a spell apparently was controlling everything: animals seemed to be drawn to Constantine Berca's rifle rather than his having to deliberately track them. Wolves were extinguished in the rifle like the light of that strange lamp. There was no other explanation for why the onslaught of the wild against the village was played out night after night by Berca's outhouses, why the whole of nature seemed to want to oust him from what was rightfully his, and why everything culminated with a thunderclap and another wolf to bury in the mound. Berca later brought home a puppy, which grew to the size of a bullock, with a pelt like sheepskin, head as big as a bushel, from which a rough, bluish tongue ever lolled. The dog also began to hunt, but this was in spring, when it throttled a polecat slinking toward the house as if in search of death, and later it would tussle with the wolves and slay them after clamping its claws and fangs. The dog had no spoken name, because his master would whistle to call it, so it knew its name by musical pitch. People had come to confuse its luck at hunting with that of Constantine Berca's, so when summer came and that woolly, white apparition began to leap over fences into any yard in the village with an air of being master of the place, paying no one any heed, neither man nor beast, its exploits had folks calling it in a way as if to explain something somehow dangerous:

"That's Constantine Berca's dog."

If someone would have wanted to deal an unexpected blow to Old Woman Fira, then the way to do it would be by introducing an unknown spell to Evil Vale. And this is just what Constantine Berca did, without even wishing it, without even thinking he would be dealing a blow to the world of spells. As the story goes, he discovered at the end of that winter the most benign way to drive off the wild beasts, more effective than all the charms ever murmured by all the stepmothers that had ever lived on that mountain. It happened when he went to Domnești to buy some long nails needed for his eternal chores with wood planks, doors, and shutters, with which he was planning to change the world. He was holding a horned club with three grooves at the tip and a metal knob fastened with tacks. No one knew how he'd arrived at such a random contraption, but this must have been his secret. Two lynxes started stalking him at the bottom of the village, ready at any step to jump on his back and suck his blood, as they're said to do when hungry, in winter, and no longer have any fear of man. Berca suddenly turned around and pointed the horned cudgel at their eyes, and the lynxes were left petrified, so that when the shepherds found them in spring they were two ashen hummocks, two moss-covered rocks. He wasn't aware at the time of what he'd done, and he never told anyone the story of the lynxes. But the gossip was that the club emitted a kind of thunderclap or ray, a kind of green emission, the color of grass, and it had sucked the life from the bodies of the lynxes and petrified them. Niculae Welldigger, who was passing by on the hill, saw it from afar and told folks in minute detail about the transformation of the wild beasts into stone, without it seeming the least bit unusual to him, for Welldigger knew a few spells of his own to turn things into stone. Old Woman Fira, who knew how to tell fortunes in grains of wheat or corn, who could cast spells with mandrake leaves or read the future in the ice on St. John the Baptist's Day, tell the future in the entrails of hens, had never in her first hundred years of life heard of a man who had so much power over nature as to be able to turn a lynx into stone.

When spring came, the folks of Evil Vale began to regard Constantine Berca as one of their own. Although now many things were being said about him, it was clear there was no point in quarreling with this man who limped, fired a gun, and knew how to cast spells with light and shoot bolts of lightning from a cudgel.

Father Dimitrie was starting to show his age. He was a man who claimed to have a vocation for souls, the gift of a true confessor, the rightful inheritor of St. Andrew the Apostle in the wild Făgăraș Mountains, cast by fate into a village with a handful of inhabitants against whose lack of faith he daily had to do battle. In his church, the hymns would rise to the heavens caressed by his deep, baritone voice, whirling through the air like hoops of sound. Midway through the service, many would grow bored and go onto the church's porch from where they would listen, a little way off, to the miracle of the transubstantiation of the bread and wine into the body and blood of Christ. After the service, the priest would also go out to the porch to tell them, to preach behind them down the village lanes:

"Look, let the black devil take this weed, didn't I tell you during the service not to drink tobacco? Didn't I tell you not to drink it?"

He had long suspected that no one in Evil Vale paid any attention to his sermons, all of them came for the hymns and for his beautiful voice, because in Evil Vale there were no musicians, nor any place where one might listen to music. This infuriated him, and he would continue his sermon anywhere he could, in the meadows, in the yards, wherever he caught them. The priest had his own theories about the world. He used to tell everyone that it was not God Who brought the war, but the Turks, their work in the world and the Ottoman Empire were the devil himself, who in olden days conquered the holy city of Constantinople, who entered the churches on horseback and emptied the holy chalices onto the ground. The priest spoke pedantically, mixing psalms with the political situation of the world then, and he tried to tie the lives of the folks of Evil Vale to the heavenly balance with bonds that only he could see.

"How can you tell the children something like that!" said Grandmother when she heard what Grandfather Berca was telling Miruna and I.

To escape Grandmother's tongue, he switched the tale to something else, and began the story of famous Baba Novac, the captain under Michael the Brave, who was of Glutton stock, one of his descendants a greedy guts who each and every day devoured an ox for lunch and by evening had slain ten Turks, but Miruna did not want to listen. She asked instead about what most interested her:

"Why is it that miracles used to happen before and today they don't happen anymore?"

Grandfather didn't know, but he told us what he did know:

"So it is. Days gone by saw one miracle after another. Today, icons no longer heal, spells no longer work."

"But why did they work back then?" Miruna asked.

There was a tale in this, too. Emerging from his first winter after receiving the plot of land, his father, Constantine Berca, learned of the terrible plague epidemic that was about to strike the land. All this happened after he had cleared away all the stones from his plot at Old Knoll, brought manure, planted saplings, and dug the earth to let it breathe. This was what he would do year after year, until the earth was transfigured and became the orchard it is today. The newspapers said the Black Death had originated in the distant land of Ethiopia, where Turkish soldiers caught it and spread it throughout Anatolia, then to Greece, and then it crossed the Danube from the battlefields of Plevna and Vidin.

There was only one hope, and only if the spells worked. Old Woman Fira cast a spell to guard against the plague, at the top of the village, using mandrake leaves and reciting from the Psalms of David, summoning and driving out all manner of invisible beings the human mind could scarcely imagine. And truth be told, the plague did not afflict the village. As Constantine Berca put it:

"Old Woman Fira's spell was a good one!"

When she heard what he'd said, Old Woman Fira bore no more grudge against him, because this, apart from his belief in the rifle and the pendulum clock, proved a faith in her powers. Her anger passed: Constantine Berca did not wish to cast spells, as Old Woman Fira had thought.

But on that Sunday, in church, after the liturgy, something unexpected happened: Father Dimitrie launched into a long sermon against witchcraft, depicting its darkness and arguing that merely the acknowledgment of spells can cause a Christian to lose his soul and to sell himself to the devil for thirty pieces of silver without even being aware of what he's doing. The priest read from the holy books and demonstrated how in the time of the Council of Nicaea lightning bolts descended from the heavens to smite the sorcerers who dotted the whole of Christendom.

"Even if on the face of it spells protect against illness," said Father Dimitrie, "even if they do good and seem to serve the truth of God, in secret, they reject the Lord and serve no one but the devil!"

On that Sunday, the weight of the word of the man of the cloth, the word of the Holy Synod of Nicaea, which excoriated witch-craft, reached Evil Vale for the first time.

Old Woman Fira, the one who used to be the mouth of the village, who cured illness and protected against wild beasts, was not often in church, although she had always felt herself to be a true believer, but the other women hastened to tell her about what had been said in the sermon. When she heard, doubt unhinged her mind. She had never expected such a blow from a servant of the Church. At first she put the priest's outburst down to his abrupt senescence, but later, wandering through her yard in the dead of night, her sleep having been shattered by cares, she decided to go without fail to confession. Had she really lived her entire life to that point in sin? All at once her entire life seemed to have been lived in error, and only now was she emerging into the light so that she could save her soul. While she truly did feel all these things, it was almost a pity to let so much skill in crafting spells go to waste, an art that was destined for the dustbin in a world so frag-mented and unwhole, a world in need of magical cures. For the most important question was this: who would now work cures? If she gave up making spells because it was a sin, who would look after people's health? And what does health have to do with faith anyway? What does medicine have to do with the Church?

Seeing that the old woman came to him full of doubt, her eyes filled with tears, the priest believed she was prepared to repent and resolved to receive holy communion and the word of Christ. A day before the fount of all evil, she received from Father Dimitrie proof of boundless understanding. He was ready to forgive all, only to bring her back onto the straight path. He started by praising the power of her spells, of which Old Woman Fira was very proud, and then he told her that confession was not possible without an understanding of her sinful deeds, and that it must commence with an elucidation of the power of the spells she knew. The old woman confessed her long-held conviction that there was nothing wrong in her casting spells and that her great error had been elsewhere, perhaps because she hadn't made all her spells with her hand on the Bible, or something of the sort. And as she also told the priest, this might be the reason why the curse of insomnia and the worms of anxiety had been awakened in her. So she said. She was fearful of something else as well: because all these spells weren't bound together in any book, they might be altered somehow, and that would be downright dangerous. It might be better to write them all down to keep them from being altered over time and working their magic the wrong way round.

"Or maybe I've mixed up who knows what spells because of old age," said Old Woman Fira, her brow pressed to the ground.

Father Dimitrie genuinely took fright. So, this was the truth, the old woman had not understood a thing. No, she must not write anything down, God forbid! Under the wing of the sacrament of confession, he told her that before the eons the devil had been a simple and undivided mind, in the likeness of the Lord, but later he severed himself from the Trinity that is higher than thought and fell into the manifold, for reasons so mysterious not even the Book of Genesis can reveal them to us, and no mention is found in the Gospels either, and thus he became a varied and much divided mind, springing up where you least suspect. It is a great wonder that in sticking your hands into one of the works or deeds of this world your fingers don't grasp the diabolical power these spells bring to light. So dispersed is the devil throughout this world that he can be found by accident just by your making a new spell, one never made before. This is not healing, it's the work of the devil.

Old Woman Fira agreed with all the priest said, as from a right-believing confessor, but she could not yet see any connection to her deeds. Referencing a handbook on witchcraft that had been donated to the church in the time of Prince Ghika, a book missing its covers and first pages, the priest then asked her:

"Is it true that you cast spells with mandrake, that you have deciphered the phantasms of sleep and foretold their meaning?"

"Yes, it is true."

"And is it true that you have read palms, that you have made spells against the evil eye and illness, that you have cast lots using the Psalms of David?"

"Yes, I have done this."

"And besides all these things, have you driven away the beasts of the forest with spells, binding the wolves and bears not to eat the cattle, and the snakes not to bite people, and moreover, have you mixed love potions for the young, who then took each other as husband and wife before the sacrament of marriage?"

"Yes, the whole world knows I do this without summoning devils, saying only the Lord's Prayer."

"And have you also told the future from the cries of birds, such as the crow and the cuckoo, also from the flight of the swallow, which is a holy bird, and have you foretold how long winter would last or how abundant the summer would be, have you cast grain on the water to scatter the clouds during haymaking, and have you reckoned by the falling stars of the night sky, claiming they were enchanted, have you told fortunes with tarot cards and in kernels of corn, beans, wheat or barley, have you quenched coals on the heads of the sick and lime at the entrance to the village to ward off the plague, have you cast spells using the small bone of a hen's leg so that the ewes will give birth to two lambs, and have you prayed to icons to grant you even more powers?"

Old Woman Fira admitted she had.

"Well, woman, all these things are deadly sins, because they are the thirteen hidden guises of the devil, and you have borne them in your body with all their cunning. You lack not a single one of them."

The old woman felt herself suffocating. She wanted to flee from the church to the ends of the earth, out of fear and shame. That her soul was lost forever, this she understood. She thought she'd come to the priest too late. She felt like weeping and could not breathe, because for a whole century she had reckoned herself a good Christian, a lover of Christ, who practiced a skill good for all things, inherited from her mother, a skill useful to the folks of Evil Vale. But Father Dimitrie clasped her by the hand and exclaimed:

"You have to escape."

She made a sign of agreement. Then the priest officiated a service like that of baptism, in which Old Woman Fira thrice said:

"I renounce Satan."

The priest next made her swear on the Holy Scriptures that she would cast no more spells or charms, neither great nor small, in order to redeem her soul and not to be hurled into the depths of darkness.

One of the first people who felt the lack of Old Woman Fira's powers was Constantine Berca, because he could have used their help in the story of Enache Mâzgău and the curse. But Old Woman Fira kept her oath. She began to concern herself solely with village gossip and with spinning yarn for coverlets and cloths, things that demand no spells of any kind. Every week she went to confession, and the priest had no peace until he heard from her own mouth that she had not cast any of the thirteen spells that for so long had been the only law in Evil Vale.

As he was working his land on Old Knoll, Constantine Berca heard a wafting, warm song, like a breeze from a season of paradise, like the unheard-of song of the fays said to come on the night of St. John's Eve to glades untrodden by human foot. Unafraid of being bound by a spell in the middle of the day, he went to have a closer look at how she passed between the blossoming plum and apple trees of that matchless spring. And he saw for the first time the cause of his troubled sleep and dreams, having no idea if she really existed. In those days, folks would run into one another just by thinking of the person. Call someone to mind, and they would appear before your eyes. It was no wonder, then, that Constantine Berca encountered her exactly as she had appeared in his dream. The wonder was that he hadn't seen her until then, as though their meeting had had to await its allotted day. She was so young that my great-grandfather thought she likely still believed in fairy tales. It is still a running joke in the family that we Bercas like our brides very young, so tender of age that they come to their wedding holding a doll. Constantine Berca saw her as she walked past and was unable to utter a word; he was unable to move from where he stood, rooted to the spot with the petrifaction he inflicted on wild beasts. All of a sudden, without pausing to think, he abandoned his chores and set off after her, like a child chasing a kite high in the sky. All the way through the blossoming apple trees the girl did not notice him for the simple reason that this wild beast of a man at war with the law of the mountain had become invisible, like a spirit in those hours of love and perdition, forgetting who he was and his name. Nor could he see the vivid colors of the world, but only a whitish mulch crisscrossed by black shadows and cold streaks. Virtually blind, like a mole, he followed the girl without her sensing it, and he saw the house she entered. Then he sat down on the grass by the edge of the road to wait for his blindness to pass. Perhaps it was at that very moment, or perhaps a good few hours had passed, when Niculae Welldigger found him, drained of thoughts and dreams, buffeted by an inner tempest.

"Who lives in the third house across the river counting from the bridge?" he asked Niculae Welldigger, "I've never known, I can't remember a house ever being there. Can it have appeared overnight?"

Niculae Welldigger told him it was Râmniceanu's place, he had received the plot of land in the time of Prince Cuza, and he had a daughter who went by the name of Domnica. Constantine Berca appareled himself in his new shirt and his best waistcoat, put a flower in his hat, and with wild eyes and fixed smile he paid a visit to Gheorghe Râmniceanu's house on the very evening of that day. He would discover later that she had been born on New Year's Eve, and that she aged only three seasons a year. After Berca tersely announced his wish to marry Domnica, Gheorghe Râmniceanu replied he had nothing against the match, except that he didn't know what the girl would say, and she was not yet able to have a say, because she was only fifteen. Râmniceanu seemed to be withholding his consent for the time being.

As the story goes, Constantine Berca returned from his courting that evening just as he went, for he had the feeling he'd been talking to someone who didn't speak the same language. In fact, a host of rumors about him had begun to travel around the village, the most frightening of which was that he could fly at night, after darkness fell, and only now did he encounter the shadow these rumors had cast. Constantine Berca was to blame for all that was said about him. Gheorghe Râmniceanu first heard about this young man from the gossip circulated by Old Woman Fira. So he had said his daughter was too young, which in his language meant no.

Constantine Berca, Miruna's great-grandfather, understood his meaning. And he swore never to think of Domnica again. This might have been his wish, but the matter had long been out of his power.

It was around this time that he called Niculae Welldigger to use his skill to look for water on his plot at Old Knoll. And Welldigger told him:

"The land they gave you is dry as old leather. It's the only parched piece of land in the whole of these mountains, it's like tinder. I've dug in other places along this slope — no water anywhere. This hill is different, it's a strange hill, like someone tossed a heap of sand from the heavens at midnight onto Evil Vale."

The skill of a welldigger is like none other because above all it requires reading the depths. Niculae had learned it from his father, after years of initiation, and his father had learned the skill from his. They searched for water using hazel twigs with the pith extracted, charmed with water from a well no one had drunk from for a whole day, so that the twigs could feel the pull of the depths. Niculae began the search by walking down the hill toward the neighboring orchard, climbing back up toward Old Knoll, slant-wise, then descending the slope once more, without receiving any sign that water was in that earth. Ultimately, Niculae had to inform Berca:

"If there's water here, then my skill isn't enough to find it."

It was his way of saying there was no water because, in the valley of Our Lady's River, the welldiggers enjoyed more trust than the priests or the spellcasters. Hearing these words, Constantine Berca's brow broke into a cold sweat. Niculae Welldigger felt his fear and sadness, for his hazel twigs leapt like a consolation in the direction of Berca's heart.

Welldigger searched a while longer, as though he himself doubted what the hazel twigs were telling him, and then he left without having found anything on the eastern slope of Old Knoll, whereupon Constantine Berca became lost in thought, gazing into the distance, down the valley as far as the high mountain that is called Nehoiu. He saw the houses of Evil Vale spread out below, white, like playthings, and the people, like dolls, slowly moving in the distance. He sat on one of the huge boulders that guarded the poorest and barest hillside in all Wallachia. From his perch he saw the gloaming of sunset, with the blue shadows descending over the foothills like cohorts of angels from a child's storybook. And for the first time in his life he was overwhelmed by the leaden weariness of those who have lost great battles. The thought that he had returned from the war only to have been granted owner-ship of barren land seemed a cruel fate. Like an ineluctable poison, sleep overwhelmed him. On that night he felt he could no longer go down into the village, that he had to sleep a heavy sleep in the arms of the orchard, with his head on one of those rocks that dotted Old Knoll, like that dimwitted giant who goes by the name of Rock Breaker, who would be overcome by sleep when you least expected it. In those days, it was not exactly wise to sleep out on the mountain with so many wolves and bears about, beasts who hadn't heard Prince Cuza's decrees that thenceforth the village was to belong to humankind. Back then the beasts of the forest did not hesitate to attack whole bands of men, let alone a sleeping man. But Constantine Berca fell asleep on the spot, without having had time to find any shelter, without thinking any more about the well or his farm, and he slept such a sleep that the dam of dreams opened and received him inside as though into a citadel, surrounding him as though in a mist with walls and towers and red shadows, like those of a latter-day Jerusalem, which will reveal itself at the end of the ages, or so it is written. The entrance to the citadel was guarded by a pair of cherubim armed with broadswords and old bandit pistols, of the kind that can crack open the padlock of heaven with a single, well-aimed bullet, girded in chain mail, their faces chiseled from stone, but living and breathing, gazing from six pairs of eyes that could encompass all the heavens and Earth. Seven maidens who had been sitting around a well in one of the citadel's gardens approached the newcomer, who was rooted to the spot. He understood the danger and wanted to flee, for cursed are those around whom gather the fays, but his legs had turned to lead, and those maidens were laughing and signaling him that only by their leave could he be released from the spell. They told him they were the emperor's daughters, and their father ruled in that castle, and Berca saw their light gait, a palm's width above the ground, and understood he was lost, for their dance had closed in around him, and it was the spirals of that ring dance that produced the spell. They caressed his brow and told him not to fear, they enticed him with perfumed fruits that do not exist on Earth, they played with his hat, tossing it back and forth between them. During this time, his hands had grown cold and no longer felt to touch, and his lips had grown hard and no longer felt to taste, and he felt his heart stopping in his breast — it was as if he had died.

"Don't you know where you are?" one of them asked. "Have you never before descended into Earth's most secret realm?"

One of them showed him the paths that branched out from there: one led to Transylvania and was narrow, like a footbridge on the lip of a chasm, a gaping depth; one led to Anatolia, the footprints of men, horses, and camels visible in the clay; and a third led to distant Egypt and was grassed over, as though no one had passed that way for a long time. All these paths were roofed by a black vault, from which streamed dark grasses, and they intersected with a white path, like a nacreous smoke, about which she said:

"The Milky Way is mirrored here. Not even we know why it looks like this."

Constantine Berca remembered some old tales about treasures buried by the hosts who had fought here with the chain-mailed armies of the right-believing Byzantine Empire. He glanced around that cave as large as a vale between two hills, looking, too, at those maidens who had gathered around him, and he understood that what he was seeing had no connection with the tales he had heard before, that this was something entirely new, something that was really happening to him. It was not a dream. It was real, for he had fallen asleep on the portal that led to this place.

One of the emperor's daughters, the one with the gift of reading thoughts, answered him:

"This is the Land of the Endless Underworld, where you will one day be called as a living man to see secrets not yet seen and to choose the path not yet chosen. That path will not be traveled by you but by the blood of your blood, in another time."

Then they began to tell him, first in a whisper, then they started to sing, then they started to dance, about the men chosen by fate to descend in dream or in madness into the distant reaches of this hidden Land, concealed in the fecund belly of Earth, where seeds sleep through winter, where apple trees gather their fruit before blossoming, and from where you can reach anywhere on Earth or in heaven by following the roots of a huge oak that draws its sap here, an oak tree from whose leaves one dream patters to another, images of faraway places, the deeps, the future, the past, images of animals not of the earth, of unseen tempests, being stored until the day of the Last Judgment. The fays lifted him up by the arms, as if he, the giant of Evil Vale, were light as a snow-flake, and they bore him toward the palace of crystal and porphyry where they had been born centuries ago. One of these creatures whispered to him that the final ruler of the world would be born in this palace, the ruler preceding the judgment of the nations, the king of the end times. The rooms of the palace, which he saw as though through a mist, dizzied by toxins and the spell, seemed to shelter the treasures of all the pirates of days gone by, for the coffers were draped with cloths of gold thread, the mirrors were plated with silver, and sitting snugly on high shelves were the four massy gold crowns of the extinct kingdoms of ages past. The room had a fresh scent of incense and basil, as though a church. Either the spell had weakened or this was merely how it had seemed to him, but he was able to move his arms, and the fays allowed him to stroke the loom of princes still unborn, whose thread, they told, held the spells of birth and fertility. If someone were to unravel the threads, all the births in the world would happen at once, simultaneously, and the end of times would be nigh. Found there were the swords of unborn knights, as well as the trumpets that would herald the end of the world, shut in glass cases with rosewood locks, so that the wind could not pass through them and no trace of their song would rise to the surface. The seven approached him in turn and told Constantine Berca about the purpose of each of those enchanted things and where each would unfold in the world. In the end, as he was beginning to feel his fingers once more, like the tingling caused by passing them through icy water, he felt pity for those in the future and fear for the fate of those alive now. He had seen war at Rahova, and that was enough for him to understand that all the things in the cave were real and they would one day sprout on Earth's surface. He knew that everything the fays told would really come to pass. They read his thoughts and laughed at him, just as you laugh at the ignorance of a child, and they told him they would lead him back to the surface and leave him to sleep at the spot whence they had taken him. They told him:

"Dig seven paces north of the place where you laid your head to sleep, believe, and there you shall find!"

Three days after they parted in the orchard, Niculae Welldigger discovered that his friend Constantine Berca had begun to dig a well all by himself and in a place the master diviner's hazel twigs had found to be of no use. Just as Old Woman Fira before, he suspected that either Berca knew a spell more powerful than the welldigger's, or his actions harbored a touch of madness. He went to the orchard to see Berca's latest outlandish deed with his own eyes, and he found him whistling a soldier's tune about the Danube and shameful things, digging twelve ells deep with a soldier's spade, a rope as thick as his arm tied around his waist to pull himself back up again. Niculae Welldigger tried to tell him that the soil was sandy on Old Knoll, that he was going about it all wrong, that the clay would swallow him up if he dug so recklessly. The soil here shifted very easily, anyone would tell you that, and the story of Master Builder Manole and his marvelous monastery built on sand was well known. Constantine Berca stopped digging and said:

"It's no longer a question of craft. With this hole I could tunnel right through the world and it still wouldn't cave in. It's a portal."

His dream had so convinced him he would find water there that he even wondered if, among other matters, it just might come gushing from the depths with such force he would be hurled into the air, and it was more from the fear of this he'd tied a rope around his waist. There can be no fooling around when a foretoken comes from the mouth of fays. Berca's faith in miracles was so entrenched that Niculae Welldigger had to speak to him as if he were whispering to someone he was trying to wake from sleep. He began by saying a few things about digging a well. Showing him that he was making no headway and, from what he could tell, was digging crookedly, that the eye of the true welldigger knows what it means to bore toward the earth's core. Managing to get Berca out of the hole, he reinforced the edges of the shaft with slabs and beams, then he began to dig, with his usual skill. He asked Berca, who was now sitting at the edge of the pit:

"How deep do you want to go before you're convinced there's no water here?"

He didn't need to dig much further until he could feel the damp, the scent, and the coolness that presaged a spring. The pocket of water came into view like an eye emerging from the depths to look at the world and to take back to the depths tidings about the sky. The greatest wonderment of Niculae Welldigger was that the water had come so close to the surface in such a sandy hill, cold and clean water such as can be found in the best wells in the vales between the foothills. He signaled Constantine Berca to pull him up, and he said:

"It's as if someone put this spring here by hand."

A few days later, Constantine Berca again put on his best clothes and crossed the river to the house of Gheorghe Râmniceanu to discuss marriage once more, with the confidence of a warrior fighting for the Ark of the Law. Over the past few days, new rumors about his deeds had stirred the whole village to thinking. It was said that he conversed with the fays and did their bidding, that he could speak to any fay without being turned to stone or being left with a crooked mouth. Whatever the case, you could not remain wholly sane after coming into their presence, because they were creatures noxious to those of human stock, noxious even when they approached men out of love. All those who saw him in the days that followed the digging of the well confessed that his eyes burned as though feverish, or like the eyes of a wild beast, that he couldn't see clearly and walk straight, as if he'd eaten something pernicious, as if he'd been poisoned. Seeing him approaching their house, Domnica ran to hide, because she had heard enough about the man. Her father could read nothing in Berca's eyes, and he didn't know if he should pay any attention to the rumors. He'd never really paid much mind to the nonsense old women concocted, nor did he believe in their spells, not even all those years ago when he saw Old Woman Fira lift a black cat into the air at midnight to release it from an illness. When Constantine Berca came once more, the very first thing Gheorghe Râmniceanu asked him was:

"What I don't understand, however hard I try, is why you're in such a rush to get married?"

And no one at that time understood Berca's haste to act, to administer justice as he saw fit on the mountain and in Evil Vale, to settle everything with human hand as though he would reverse all the world's locks. Râmniceanu didn't understand anything of what he had heard or seen of Constantine Berca either. Back then, time was infinite and haste was relatively unknown.

Berca tried to explain, to tell the story of the large, fruitful orchard he was going to make on Old Knoll, he began to tell of the land given by the king, but the words that came from his mouth sounded strange, like the Slavonic liturgy Father Svetoslav recited at the Pasărea Monastery, which no one could understand.

Gheorghe Râmniceanu told him once again to think of Domnica's age, and to show him what he meant, he called Domnica to come out. As soon as she came up to them by the gate, he asked her if she wanted this man for a husband.

The girl remained silent, looking into Constantine Berca's

eyes, her face etched only with fury. All of a sudden, she looked up haughtily, more determined than ever, and answered curtly:

"No, I don't."

"You see?" said Gheorghe Râmniceanu, "she doesn't."

Berca frowned and looked at her with eyes that seemingly saw her for the first time. He heard her say to him:

"I've heard things about you I don't like."

Berca recalled that village gossip was all too real, and in Evil Vale rumors have more power than the fays. The rumors ran up and down the length of Our Lady's River, from village to village, borne by shepherds, peddlers, and the wind until they came to bind a man forever.

"And you believe what they say about me?"

"What folks say," said Domnica, "has always been true."

This annoyed Constantine Berca to no end, because he'd always felt that the world of women was hemmed in by an impassable wall. Domnica told him what the girls were saying about him, that the old women were recalling distant events involving his father which seemed similar to what he was experiencing, and then she said what they all suspected:

"They say you're not quite right in the head, that maybe you lost your mind in the war."

Instead of flying into a rage, Berca started to laugh when he heard this:

"Is that all?"

Then, as though taking it seriously:

"So, you think I'm mad, like Elifterie from the brandy still?"

First she smiled, showing no trace of doubt, and then nodded her head.

"So if I'm mad," said Constantine Berca, "who else is there for you to marry?"

"There are other boys and plenty of time."

At this point, Gheorghe Râmniceanu thought this man with the unhinged mind would go away and never come back, neither to ask for his daughter's hand nor on any other business, defeated not so much by Domnica's words as much as by pride. And, indeed, only a few moments passed before he looked at her with those burning eyes and said all in one breath:

"Why would I not be in my right mind? What sort of nonsense have they been saying? Tell me what you've heard and then I'll tell you what's true."

Domnica replied:

"Word has been going around that you spent all your pay from the war on a German clock with springs and pendulums, which sits on the wall and chimes the hour, like in a boyar's house. And rumor has it that at night you can't sleep and you wander through the garden and change into a winged man or something else, and that's why you carry an old rifle, which you use to shoot wolves and foxes so they won't steal your secret from the clock, when you want to transform yourself, or maybe because it's part of a spell. And they say you got water from dry rock, digging in a dry place on the Knoll, and others say you're so strong and so wild you once killed a bear in the woods with your bare hands. And they say you're a kind of wizard, the last wizard in these mountains, the one who gathers together all their powers and discovers spells for himself one by one, and who does unheard-of things. And they say the fays teach you what to do. Folks don't know why you do all these things, because all of this come together in a single man is something never seen before."

Berca smiled, and rather than answer to all the things she said, replied in a clipped voice:

"What about you? What kind of husband would you like? Would you like a man who can't do any of these things?"

She felt a cold mist descend upon her, and she thought this was a new spell he was preparing to cast. Though Domnica's parents could not see or sense a thing, a full battle of vortices and preternatural powers had begun as if pitting someone who wanted to steal Domnica and take her far away against someone who was trying to keep her in her childhood place. So the story goes, and so it was. She gave a start, and on the other side of that instant her face was transformed into that of a young woman's. This is where we began, Grandfather told Miruna, this is when all our family came into being, all those who are of Berca blood in Evil Vale, because it is said that the fays taught their chosen man a certain spell, and so the line was born. Domnica is supposed to have smiled, all of a sudden she changed, and then she said yes. The tale does not tell us how much longer they talked that day, but a spell seems to have been at work as the wedding was set for the beginning of winter, around the end of November. And a year after the wedding they were blessed with their first-born, a son, Gheorghe. Then came Ioan. Then Mara, the girl whose face bore the sign of love and whose beauty did not come from this world. And the last of the brood was Niculae, who preserved the stories until they came down to us, that is, Grandfather, who handed down the stories to us and told us that his father was protected in love by the unbinding spell of the fays.

When Grandfather fell silent, Miruna's eyes sought Mother and Father, who were also there, listening. And Mother asked Grandfather:

"Why are you telling them such things? They're too little and can't understand. You told them to us when we were much older, and never the complete story as you've been telling them now."

"I see them with different eyes now," said Grandfather. "It's because they haven't experienced anything yet that this seems like a story to them. My feeling is that all these events had no other purpose than for their tale to be told right now."

Miruna was glad to hear this. She was sitting on the bench by the gate, by her grandfather, wearing the jerkin from Grandmother. I was looking at her, and I remember that I could hardly believe that one day we would grow up. It seemed a lie to me, a kind of punishment to threaten us with, and we wanted to know more, we wanted his stories, the ones from the world he grew up in, whereupon he told us the most bizarre tale of all.

"I am going to tell you the only story that has ever terrified me." It happened long ago, at the time when as many of the sheepfolds as there still are today had begun to pack up for the winter. At the Mohorea sheepfold, right beneath Mount Nehoiu, which can be seen on clear days from our yard, on that side to the north, there was a shepherd from Săliște by the name of Andreiaș Gozgu. No wild beast of the forest had ever got the better of that man, which is to say he had never lost any sheep or lamb. This was his fame, and they brought him from Mărginime to shepherd the flocks from Evil Vale. His fame as a skilled and lucky sheep breeder had spread far and wide. One night, wolves were glimpsed in the woods near the Mohorea sheepfold, where another six shepherds were with Andreiaş Gozgu, and their flocks were penned, with dogs tied at the gates, and the mules were tethered to stakes behind the fold. At night they heard the howl of an old, hungry wolf nearby, and more howls resounded in the valley, wolves that dared come no closer. They were many. Even though the packs disperse in summer, only hunger gathers them together again, so that they end up prowling around the sheepfolds when they do not manage to catch a deer or some other game. Some shepherds grabbed clubs, some axes, to go out and fend off the wolf.

"You stay inside. I'll take care of the wolves," said Andreiaş Gozgu.

They looked at one another and thought the man reckless to rely on his luck. But who knows what madness took hold of them, and they did not follow, they left him to drive away the wolves on his own, thinking he would use some spell like the one Berca used to turn lynxes to stone. And he did not take a cudgel, he took nothing, not even throwing a mantle over his shoulders, but went out of the sheepfold hut wearing only his shirt. The shepherds inside waited for a few moments, amazed at how Andreiaş Gozgu would drive away the wolves, recalling to mind all they had heard about spells for warding off, about charms and mysterious enchantments, when all of a sudden from near the sheepfold they heard a bloodcurdling howl, loud and sharp, that of a young wolf in the prime of its strength. They froze one and all, and they imagined Andreiaş Gozgu face to face with the wolf. Then silence, and they had no idea what was happening, they heard no more movements in the darkness outside, not even the dogs baying. Andreiaş Gozgu came back inside and told them they could now sleep easy. Perhaps this was how the rumor started that the man's sheep did not get eaten because he could converse with the wolves in their own tongue, and, what is more, he had the throat of a wolf, or a certain power of changing into a wolf on nights of a full moon and white moonbeams, like the sky at the beginning of the world. And folks trembled, especially when on another night, also at the Mohorea sheepfold, Gozgu went outside at midnight during a full moon, and without the dogs sensing him or anyone hearing any sign, it was rumored he tore apart six sheep belonging to his fellow shepherds and ate their hearts, leaving them ripped open next to the flock. So the story went. No one dared say anything to him in the light of day, not knowing what powers were latent in him, but all knew the truth having seen him grown fat and groggy overnight as though after a bandits' wassail. Only Gheorghe Fruntașu, a shepherd from Rucăr, who knew the ways of the place, dared confront him:

"Hey, Andreiaș, what's with them sheep?"

Gozgu said nothing, but the man from Rucăr asked again:

"Why did the wolves only tear apart our sheep but didn't touch yours?"

Gozgu then replied with a wan smile:

"Just lucky I guess!"

For a long time the truth of it was not known. Some said that the man could turn into a wolf, and others that nothing of the like was possible, because nothing of the kind was mentioned in any of the holy books. How could one creature transform into another? And it was also at the Mohorea sheepfold, which is not far from the village, that Andreiaș Gozgu just so happened to go out one night during a full moon at the time when Constantine Berca had nothing better to do than hunt wolves at the bottom of his garden, on one of those nights when he would go out to bring the wilderness under the rule of man, and so saw by the gate by the river a large wolf with a white collar like a king's ruff, and was amazed at such an unprecedented apparition. Berca aimed well and shot once, hitting the wolf between the eyes.

At the Mohorea sheepfold they did not know what to believe when at dawn there was no trace of Andreiaș Gozgu, and not the following day either. Then the shepherds spread out to search for him in the woods and on the mountain. An old man set off for the village of Evil Vale to ask the folks if they'd seen Gozgu from Săliște. On the following evening, they found Constantine Berca flaying the largest wolf that had ever been hunted in the Făgăraș Mountains. The old man saw the animal hanging by the legs behind Berca's gate by the main road and recognized at first sight the eyebrows and eyes of Andreiaș Gozgu and the white collar, as though it were the Săliște woollen mantle he was wearing on his shoulders when he left the sheepfold never to return. The wolf looked so much like Andreiaș there could be no doubt that the madman of Evil Vale had gunned down the emperor of the wolves. The shepherds held council and decided that the best thing would be to keep quiet about the incident to the gendarmes, because the lawmen never understood the way things worked in these mountains. In fact, Berca had shot him at an hour when he was a wolf, so it was a wolf he killed, and that was of no concern to the law. So ended the tale for the shepherds, but Constantine Berca's soul was deeply troubled. He swore he would never shoot anything at night again; he then went to church to pray for Andreiaș Gozgu's soul, as he felt he would be considered guilty of murder at the Last Judgment, along with the twenty-one pagans in their human guise he shot during the Battle of Rahova. This shooting would weigh more heavily at the Last Judgment as it was the slaying of a mountain brother, even if the killing occurred while he'd been transformed into a wolf. Father Dimitrie found him by the icons and asked him if he had ever enchanted his rifle. Yes, replied Constantine Berca, he had carved three notches on the butt and recited the Lord's Prayer. Berca then made confession to Father Dimitrie, and the priest had him swear he would never again use spells. The priest read the list of the thirteen guises of the devil to him as well, and he asked Berca to renounce them.

2

Grandfather was sitting beside us on the bench, unfolding the latest issue of that dreary Party newspaper *The Spark*, of which he did not believe a jot. He was reading about the formation of a new coalition cabinet in Italy, the floods in China, and the latest eruption of Krakatoa, which sits on the lip of hell. Miruna watched him as he read, following his eyes through the thick lenses of his spectacles, and she understood how far removed Grandfather was from all the things written in the newspaper. Why then did he read them if they were so distant from him? The first pages of *The Spark* that day contained an entire speech by comrade Nicolae Ceaușescu, a speech no one would read, having no story, in unbroken newsprint save some photographs reminiscent of school graduation ceremonies, leaving Miruna and I to conclude that it must be something about the awarding of an important prize, meaning nothing to us.

The wind ran its fingers through the garden by the house, and the evening tinted the distant mountains blue. I knew which of them was Mount Nehoiu: Grandfather had pointed it out to me on the horizon. I recall those evenings with their scent of repose, when everything would be plunged into consummate silence. I would try to imagine how our great-grandfather's flintlock must have sounded in that silence of old. Whenever Miruna would play, running beneath the branches of the trees, the scattered rays of the sun among the leaves just bursting into bloom, whatever the season of the year, the light seemed to us to reverberate with the tinkle of enchanted bells. This was the hour when you could feel that time did not flow in one direction but rather whirled in place like a spinning top dropped by the Gentle Ones, the legendary gymnosophists who dwell at the ends of the earth, on the banks of the River Saturday, and who measure the flow of eternity — a top that had been spinning from the very first hour of the world, repeating, without change, all things from the very beginning.

As that summer was winding down, another wind-colored vortex rose from the whirl of Grandfather's memory, and he read to us from it as if it were an ancient tome.

This time, the tale took place back when His Majesty King Carol wanted everyone to speak about him all the time and, if possible, to say only good things. A girl and three boys had been born to Constantine Berca by then, and he needed more and more things for his household. So he took up woodworking. Most of the time he relied on his own devices, just as he had done when he dug the well, and his hands fashioned things in the way they were meant to be. In those days, all the folks of Evil Vale were making good money working the timber of those mountains.

It was years before the forestry laws were enacted, and all the men along Our Lady's River would go to market with their boards, planks, and barrel wood. There was so much wood in the forests of Muscel that the exodus of tree trunks down Our Lady's River or by cart to the towns of the plain didn't seem to trouble the woods. Constantine Berca decided to sell his lumber in Bucharest, where the price was good and a lot of building work was going on. He went to the forest, and with axe and hatchet, all by himself, he worked so much lumber that he could have girdled the whole of Bucharest with his boards. He knew how to make planks for furniture, which are different from planks for floorboards, and he also knew how to make gateposts and roof shingles — anything a building boom in the city might require.

At that time, however, the road to Bucharest through the Vlăsiei Forest was barred by the bandits led by the notorious Oarţă Aman, the most fearsome of all the forest chieftains who has ever had his story told. The exploits attributed to Oarţă Aman were more terrible than those told about the Tartars of lore. Mothers would frighten their children with Oarţă Aman the bandit, not with ogres or steel-beaked woodpeckers. His band fought fearlessly in the forest or in the open field, against posses or gendarmes, and would always either emerge triumphant or vanish without a trace. When there was nothing for them to prey upon in the forest, they would go into the town in disguise, stealing with a delight that put their lives in danger at any given moment, for their faces were now known to the gendarmes. And they feared for their lives not one whit, they were all exceptional, each had been in jail at one time or another, and two of them had been sentenced to hang but escaped from their guards, as can only happen in Wallachia. Oarţă Aman, it was said, had been a captain in the war against the Turks and had taken part in the Battle of Vidin, where his own hand had mown down four hundred and sixty-two of the enemy, unprecedented deeds for which he had been decorated four times in the winter of the war. He was the son of a boyar, and his family's estate was on the plain, but the threads of the tales about him were very tangled. Some said he'd drunk his fortune away because of his heartbreak over a Greek woman who they say left him for an Italian merchant. Others said that when he came back from the war he'd been disinherited by his father for a forbidden love affair, a liaison with an impoverished princess of the Știrbey line. Out of rage, so the rumors went, the soul of Oarță Aman was transformed and, having seen the face of war at Vidin, he found nothing better to do now that he had left his home, no matter the reason, than to take to the woods. He was bloodier for having become a bandit not to get rich, as was the case with his cohorts, but because there was nothing left for him to do in life. Domnica learned this story down to the very last strand of hair from Old Woman Fira, who told it to her as soon as she learned of Constantine Berca's plan to make quick money selling his lumber in Bucharest. Delighted that she knew all the details of this old story, Old Woman Fira spread it throughout the village. She began by telling it to the wife of innkeeper Constantine Dulubaș, who generally passed on all she heard. The story was believed at once and borne further on the wind down the Argeș Valley and the Topolog Valley, so that the very next day the whole world began to fortify their doors with iron bars and double bolts, to padlock their cellars and to wall up their dowry coffers, because the arrival of the bandits was expected at any moment. Constanine Berca pretended to have heard nothing of the rumors that were circulating. He knew that wild tales came with autumn and the many lies told in the Făgăraș Mountains. He loaded his cart with lumber and prepared plenty of shot for his rifle, just in case. And he jammed his trusty powder horn into his girdle, a handy receptacle for that ancient flintlock, which, according to the merchant who sold it to him, had been in the Crimean War. His only thought was to get to Bucharest and quickly find a buyer with whom he could deal for years to come. Domnica begged him to change his mind, because Oarță Aman was real, not just an old wives' tale from the Vlăsiei Forest.

"There is no Oarță Aman," Constantine Berca answered her, stroking her cheek. "Not one of the tales about him can be believed. They're all just stories for children."

Domnica did not give up easily. She reminded him that everything Old Woman Fira said proved to be true in the end. In fact, if he thought about it, the price of lumber in Argeș or Câmpulung was not that bad. Why not go there? She told him it was pointless to take his gun, for Oarță Aman was not like a wolf one could aim at, his eyes did not gleam in the dark, and Aman's rifle was new and his aim ten times better than the best marksman in Evil Vale. That was how he had got the better of so many posses sent by the king. He stole the horses from under the gendarmes and emptied the pockets of the lords traveling by carriage to Bucharest. Oarță Aman was not just anybody: he had been to war and knew how life mixed with death.

Her pleas were futile. Berca was convinced that all those stories amounted to nothing more than the nonsense of women. Listening to her talk, he became enraged that women would give credence to such common rumors, but his ire subsided the more he listened, changing first to incredulity, then to tenderness. Still, nothing could turn him from his path.

Then she said to him:

"You know, I sense you're going to see death on this journey and come face to face with a funeral. But it won't be an ordinary one."

Magic likely was involved, though Domnica had no desire to tell him about it. She had read the future, seen the shadow of a future day full of darkness and death, yet she didn't know everything, or she didn't wish to tell him everything she'd seen. Constantine Berca understood this, but only after he'd set off to the blacksmith's, leading his stallion by the bridle. He was readying to leave all the same. He thought about the presentiment women have of danger, how they have something within, likening them to the sentinels of the heavens who see ahead in time. Or was this, too, merely a silly tale?

Constantine Berca could never be turned back from his path, not then, not ever. He left on a Thursday, at sunrise, and by midday he had reached an inn at the edge of Pitești, where there were other men with carts laden with tons of cheese, timber, lambs, fatted hens, and vegetables the like of which had not been grown in Vlașca County all that year. There were goods of every variety, an entire fair assembled at the inn. They discussed traveling through the forest together, so that the bandits would not have the courage to attack them. At dawn, they agreed that the front and the rear of the convoy should have two carts, not one, with men armed with axes, and in the column there would also be three or four who had rifles. As the first cart set off, just a glance at the warlike aspect of this rustic convoy made plain what renown Oarță Aman had gained as captain of the bandits. Everything had been planned and prepared according to the ancient rules of medieval battle. Amazed that no one attacked them in the forest, they saw as the reason their skill in stringing together twenty carts as if a military maneuver, like the Macedonian phalanx described in the *Romance of Alexander*, not that they were just lucky. The only thing on this road to cause Constantine Berca any fear was the depth and density of the forest, darker than the darkest mountain wood, so black that not a single ray of light pierced it. Such was the Vlăsiei Forest back then, on black and fruitful earth in the middle of the plain, wild and lawless. They entered Bucharest by night on the Chitila side, accompanied by a wind from afar, which had kept pace with them as they approached the city. That sweet-scented wind had also crossed the plains and hills, had caressed the sources of rivers and was now brushing the silver clappers of the three hundred bells fading in the last sounds of dusk. Later, in the depths of night, the bells of the Church of St. John the Baptist slipped their wooden stays and rang out loudly to warn of fire, and so it was that Constantine Berca heard them for the first time as he lay sleeping by his cart at the edge of the city. That night, Great-grandfather Berca did not dream.

He quickly wrapped up his business in Bucharest, having sold the wood to a merchant in the Obor Market for a good price, and then set off back to the mountains with the money in his girdle. At the edge of Bucharest, he saw a number of men gathered by their carts, waiting after being stopped by the army, who informed them that posses had set out from the garrisons that morning and were now combing the forest for bandits. A few days before in the Royal Council the king recalled the promise he had made twenty years ago upon arriving in Wallachia to rid the place of bandits.

For the king, the Vlăsiei Forest seemed so close to his palace that he could no longer conceal his anger at the lawlessness that besieged the bastions of order and civilization. The men said he had summoned his Minister of War and generals and commanded them to deploy an entire army to encircle the forest whence the bandits emerged to pillage. Then the cavalry made its first charge against the unseen, that is, against such an impenetrable cover as the forest. The soldiers combed every blade of grass over vast swathes of woods, searching every dell and knoll until they managed to surround all the bandits, together with their captain, Oarță Aman, in the place known as Stags' Mound. It was there the battle took place. The bandits were of no mind to entertain any notion of surrender. Some were carrying money and jewels, strings of gold coins and waistcoats weighted down with rouleaux of Napoleons — all that Oarță Aman gave them the last time they had divvied up the loot, all they had not had time to bury in their hideaways. Each knew that if caught he would end up before a firing squad. So they fought like true warriors. In the first moments of the battle the voice of their captain, Oarță Aman, could be heard exhorting them to fight, and the voices of some of them were heard responding. They knew there was no other choice. Unaware of the size of the posse arrayed in the woods, they could not know that they were caught in the steely vise of a will more obdurate than any thus far seen in Wallachia. They'd had the impertinence to attack the gendarmes and army patrols, but now it was the soldiers' turn to attack them, forcing them to stand and fight. The shooting lasted no more than half an hour, and some claimed that the last bandit at large was Oarță Aman himself, who refused to be captured alive. The story goes that he removed his right boot and pulled the trigger of his rifle with his toe, discharging the barrel under his chin. He had a German long rifle, the range and accuracy of which was known far and wide. His last shot rendered his face unrecognizable, because the soldiers took all the dead bodies and laid them by the side of the road, at which point the commissars came with their files to identify them. But the face of Oarţă Aman was nowhere to be seen. Then the army allowed the carts of those returning from market and waiting for the battle to end to continue on their way toward the mountains, among them Constantine Berca with his empty cart. He saw all the bodies lying at the edge of the road, each one with a shot to the chest or the forehead. He said nothing of this at home for more than twenty years, but he was convinced that Domnica's premonitions had come true, because she had spoken to him of the approach of death, and so it had been. He waited many years before he told the tale of the terrifying moment of identifying the corpses to his son Niculae, describing how the commissars stood there, ledgers in hand, looking over the dead and saying:

"This is Oarţă Aman, because he has a hooked nose and jutting chin."

"No, this one is, because he has prominent cheekbones and we know he took after his Tartar grandmother."

"No, it's neither of those two, gentlemen. Oarţă Aman is this one here, who shot himself."

The commissar pointed at a corpse with open eyes, which even in death preserved the arrogance of the captain of the robbers.

No two of the commissars identified one and the same Oarţă Aman. Each of the bodies had enough resemblances to be the bandit captain and enough differences to place any positive identification in doubt.

When the tale reached this point, Grandfather heard Miruna's voice suddenly say:

"Grandpa, please tell me a story where no one dies."

The tide of memories ebbed, faded, and, cast into the depths by the whirlwind stirred up by Miruna's request, completely vanished. And it changed into a story for children, one that sprouted like a tendril from the real stories of times gone by, then another tendril from legends and early ballads. From the remnants of spells and stories Grandfather improvised an original version of the fairy tale "Unaging Youth and Deathless Life," at the end of which Prince Charming no longer sets foot in the forbidden Vale of Tears, no longer pines away for his family, and abandons the castle of immortality, but lives happily ever after with the three unaging and deathless princesses, and they all love each other with the heart of a child. Miruna listened carefully to Grandfather's tale and then said:

"Hold on a minute, Grandpa! You're getting them mixed up! That's not the way it goes . . . I think you've forgotten the story . . ."

Grandfather looked at her as if seeing her for the first time. There was no way Miruna could know it, but a story where something or other didn't turn to dust was simply not possible. Or a story where no one died. And Miruna wouldn't have believed such a story, even though she'd requested it . . . Grandfather must have thought she wouldn't be able to distinguish lifelike stories from those having nothing to do with this world. He thought her capable of fully understanding only fairy tales about Prince Charming and Ileana Cosânzeana, but even here ogres do what they do and eventually work their way into the story, though in altered guise, so as to bolster the expected happy ending. Grandfather's stories still had some spice in them because they had long ago crossed the boundary set for a bedtime story. Is it appropriate to tell children about all the sad and terrifying events of the past? To Niculae Berca's mind, the tales he told us should not exclude such things. Grandfather remembered that when he first heard the tale of the Battle of Rahova from his father he'd been unable to sleep that night. As soon as he closed his eyes, he would be visited by the headless dead, by men without mouths or noses, walking with gaping, filthy wounds, a hand sprouting in place of the head, wounded arms reaching out as if begging. Such stories have something in them, as if holding you in their sway. They cross over into dream, and from dream back into reality. Around the same time, on another evening, as Grandmother was combing Miruna's hair and Grandfather had just finished his newspaper with its truncated news reports, the string of memories brought to the surface another strange story. It happened long ago, a long, long time ago. Once upon a time ago.

The German's pendulum clock kept watch over Constantine Berca's nights, its church-bell chime thrusting the silence heavenward and measuring the hours between dreams. Wild beasts prowled through the village at night, but nary one through the yard where so many wolves lay buried. After one such a night, Constantine Berca found Elifterie from the brandy still in his yard, sleeping peacefully on the steps, dressed in rags of untold age, with a long, white beard full of teasel, his blue eyes lost in infinite grogginess. The dog had not barked, as if he had not sensed him. Berca looked at him as if seeing him for the first time. He was so old and grimy it was obvious he hadn't washed since before he lost his memory. Now he lived on the charity of the folks in Evil Vale, hiding during winter in one of the communal buildings, where an ancient stove made of stones kept him warm. Everything he wore, as well as his words, had been donated to him, for he never spoke with his own words, only regurgitated the words of someone else, repeated snatches of speech, perhaps from the day before, perhaps from times long past. His eyes were set deep in his head and his gaze was fixed — Old Woman Fira used to say this was the unmistakable sign of someone who had come close to the fays. Constantine Berca saw in Elifterie a brother, though one less fortunate, a wanderer in this world, lost on this earth, driven out of that magical land in the deeps whose beauties had obnubilated his mind. Old Woman Fira also used to say that he'd been left like this one day at work, when he was still a lad, after he had cut himself with a scythe and lost so much blood that his senses were turned upside down. He had fled toward the river, where wounds are cleansed and closed when bound with the right herbs, but it was at midday, and he encountered six enchanted fays bathing in the waters of Our Lady's River, in the waterfall at the end of Evil Vale. Their nacreous bodies, their inhuman pearly eyes, their lips that glowed from within were more than any man could stand to behold. Elifterie awoke near nightfall, alone in a meadow, his wounds having been tended, receiving in return that forgetting without cure, in whose grip he had forever remained. In the space of a single day he had become an old man, wary, ill-suited to the world, overwhelmed by a sadness he could not comprehend.

Yet Constantine Berca had been in that realm, too, he had seen it, he knew it, and he had returned whole. Even though Elifterie frightened his youngest child, Niculae, Constantine Berca let him stay in his yard, and as winter was coming, made him a coat and gave him one of his shirts. Elifterie sat in the little room off the kitchen and would sleep only on straw, a kind of nest that he'd made for himself as though by a spell. His goodwill seemed to overcome his clumsiness, all the more so given that no one ever asked him to do any chores. Elifterie was so helpless it was truly a miracle he had survived and managed to reach such an advanced age. No one in the village had ever thought to do for him what Constantine Berca hadn't hesitated to do. After Old Woman Fira had informed everyone about Elifterie's new life, they all felt somehow relieved. Berca's surprise was all the greater given what happened next. One day the following spring, while climbing the hill to the orchard he came across Enache Mâzgău, who stopped him to inquire if it were true that he had given Elifterie refuge in his house. What Enache Mâzgău then said to him no one would ever know, although according to village gossip he said Berca was a bastard who'd been raised thanks to the mercy of the innkeeper, and his real father was none other than Elifterie. At least this is what folks said transpired. If these were indeed his words, then no one should wonder that Constantine Berca, who was quick to anger, abruptly took him by his shirt collar and shouted that he knew who his father was.

"That's what you think," laughed Mâzgău.

Still holding him by the collar, Constantine Berca then glimpsed something unknown to his eyes, something from who knows where: maybe it was hatred, maybe pride, in any case it carried a whiff of perdition. The man was angered by all the changes Berca had brought to village ways. Every new thing village gossip told about Berca roused him to anger, and the story about Elifterie must have topped them all, although clearly it had nothing to do with him. There was no need for hidden motives, the anger was palpable, the fury had been lying in wait, nothing more was required. Having read this in the man's eyes as he was holding him up by the scruff of the neck, at eye level, Berca flung him to the ground hard enough to bury him up to the knees in the sand of the orchard slope. Calmed as if by a miracle, he asked:

"What's it to you?"

Enache Mâzgău laughed as if he thought himself safe and said Berca had no reason to be so high and mighty, with his rifle and his pendulum clock, because they, the village folk, knew who he was — a man from nowhere who kept company with men from nowhere.

Then a strange thing happened. Constantine Berca uttered a curse for the first time in his life, without giving much thought that the fays might hear it. He wished illness on Enache Mâzgău. The curse descended into the earth, into the water table of the orchard, then it flowed through the subterranean darkness until it reached the roots of the mountains. The curse traveled its course into the depths and there came to a stop, and this is where the fays heard it.

Welldigger sensed in his divining rods that a fissure, or a silence, or a forgetting, was about to yawn open, the same as he sensed when someone was losing his mind. Something told him it involved Constantine Berca. He kept his composure, and when they met at dusk in front of his house, he told Berca that some men weren't like others, men who've returned from the wuthering depths transform into something else, like metamorphoses in fairy tales. It is not just a matter of ogres transforming themselves into birds, but of men transforming themselves into snakes and all manner of mutation. Welldigger also told him that a man is never just a man; he carries with him something else besides. The return from the wuthering depths and transformations always entail much more than what we can see in the light of day.

When Constantine Berca told him about the noontime encounter, Welldigger was also at a loss to explain what had happened in the heart and mind of Enache Mâzgău. The event had no meaning, it made no sense, it was unconnected to any other event till then.

Yet the thought that he might be a bastard haunted Constantine Berca for many days. He felt more at peace after talking with Niculae Welldigger, but the thought that he knew nothing about his birth began to accompany the thought that he bore the sin of his curse, for he had cursed in anger, and this caused him a sleepless night. Fever took hold of him. For Domnica it was a night of anguish, because she did not know how to care for a man who was experiencing such an intense nightmare. In the heat of the fever, wiping the sweat from his brow and his chest, Domnica listened to him tell what tortured his mind, and the next morning, when Constantine Berca opened his eyes and gazed upon the light of a new day, he saw Father Dimitrie at his bedside. The priest had brought a book of hours and was reading from it in a whisper. When he saw the sick man open his eyes, he said:

"I heard what you said. You are not a bastard child. The claim is baseless. I baptized your father and I knew your father. Elifterie arrived in Evil Vale many years after your birth. All these things are nonsense, and though these words left you broken-hearted, it is now time for you to get out of bed."

Father Dimitrie had no way of knowing the true cause of Constantine Berca's fever. Even though Berca was unaware of what he'd been saying, he hadn't forgotten. Old Woman Fira was the one who sussed everything out. That morning she awoke, washed her eyes, thrice made the sign of the cross, and began a new day of weaving at the loom, as had been her wont since she renounced magic spells. But overnight her threads had become so tangled that the shuttle sprang back three times when she tried to tamp down the first thread. At which point she bent down and read in the threads of the loom, because that tangle conveyed a message.

It was a curse. Old Woman Fira knew it. Someone in Evil Vale had released a curse, and it had been heard, the deepest curse from these parts in a long time, it had descended to the roots of the mountain, its words were now at work, it was too late for anyone to stop it. Only for such reasons do threads tangle themselves overnight.

Constantine Berca was ashamed to confess all to Father Dimitrie. Even though nothing had happened yet, all those who had read the signs knew the story would not end well.

Meanwhile, Enache Mâzgău hadn't been idle either. He went to the gendarmes with proof that Constantine Berca was preparing an uprising in the mountain villages against the Monarchy, against the tax collectors and the rulers, especially now that a new timber law was said to be in the offing. These years were the most turbulent for Romanian villages. The gendarmes were terrified of uprisings, and every rumor was thought to conceal a grain of truth. So at exactly the hour when Father Dimitrie was soothing Constantine Berca and reading to him from the book of hours, three mounted gendarmes were entering Evil Vale to take him all the way to Câmpulung for questioning.

Yet once again events were to take a different course. The gendarmes discovered in Evil Vale something so unusual that they forgot about the peasant and his uprising and hurried back to their commandant to report that no one in the village, or in the surrounding villages, had any legal documentation, because the administrative services had completely forgotten about the existence of these hamlets. There were thousands of people without legal documents. Moreover, the area was still using coins from the time of Prince Ghika, and the only unit of measure they knew was the *oka* from the time of Alexandru Cuza. Instead of identity papers, people used war veteran certificates, and when selling each other land they exchanged *chrysobulls*, or golden bulls, from the time of Matei Basarab. The news caught up with the prefect of Muscel County as he was taking his afternoon coffee and reached Bucharest by cable that evening. When His Excellency the Minister of Home Affairs found out that in Muscel there were whole villages omitted from the official records, he exclaimed:

"We are geniuses at survival and hopeless at administration."

When folks in Evil Vale spoke of legal acts, they thought only of military discharges and the deeds to hay meadows and orchards, which is to say, the documents they kept rolled up next to the icon and that were more authentic the older they were. Marriages were recorded in the church register and nowhere else. No one had identity papers or marriage certificates, and no one issued birth certificates because the whole village was governed by a legal code from the time of an apocryphal prince who had governed Wallachia from a nearby manor for one week two hundred years ago but had left in his wake all kinds of administrative customs that were still in use by force of tradition solely in that corner of the country. What's more, a few of the Evil Vale villagers who spoke with the gendarmes were convinced that Alexandru Ioan Cuza was still king, and one of them, aged and toothless, was even convinced the gendarmes had been sent by order of Prince Ştirbey. Over the course of the following weeks, when the populace of Evil Vale, Sân Andrei, Slatina, and a handful of other villages was registered, the number of the country's inhabitants at once increased by ten thousand souls whose existence no one had ever suspected. This administrative anomaly then came to the attention of His Royal Majesty, and the subject began to fascinate him.

Enache Mâzgău never did understand why the authorities brought their investigations into the matter of preparing for revolt in Evil Vale to a close so quickly. Nor did he understand the alacrity with which notaries and ledger-bearing tax collectors canvassed the village from top to bottom, nor why the village gossip had not foretold of it.

Yet village gossip did have something to say about it. In spite of the curse that held Enache Mâzgău in its thrall, his farm fared better than any other in the village. His flock of sheep had multiplied very quickly, and the shingles and tiles made by his son, Toader, were the most in demand at market. Everything was going as well as could be until the day when Mâzgău slaughtered one of the suckling pigs on his farm and made merry all Sunday long with his kinfolk. It may well be that the meat was tainted, though Enache Mâzgău wasn't the only one who ate it. But he was the only one to take ill. This happened the week Ioan the kite-maker, a man whose lifelong wish was that he'd been born a bird, discovered the secret of becoming airborne and managed to lift himself aloft from the Knoll using a mechanism made entirely of wood, with parts fitted together without nails and glued with a light resin. Perhaps his mind had long been wandering in a whirl having more to do with the archangels than with the fays, for he had paid no mind to the secret of returning to the earth. So in gentle flight he rose in his contraption, which looked like a windmill, over Petrașcu's yard, then over Enache Mâzgău's outhouses, until he disappeared into a curtain of cloud near Mount Nehoiu, deep into the mountains, somewhere over Transylvania, to where go all who wish they'd been born with wings. A few days after that Sunday, without any prior warning, Enache Mâzgău was stricken with dreadful stomach pains, and in a few weeks his belly swelled until it was fit to burst. He was nauseous, like a pregnant woman, his face was as yellow as maize, his legs had grown thin, and his jowls drooped, while his belly grew a finger's width daily, until it was so big he could no longer get it through the door of his house.

"This is the curse of Constantine Berca," village gossip concluded. "He knows how to curse, and his words have weight."

Father Dimitrie examined Old Woman Fira, making her answer his questions with her hand on the Bible, suspecting her of being mixed up in a deed so terrible as the fulfillment of a curse. But Old Woman Fira didn't need to be mixed up in it to tell him there was no remedy in the world — be it sanctioned or outlawed by the Church — that could save Enache Mâzgău now. And it was no work of hers — of that the priest could be assured.

Enache Mâzgău's suffering was so great that his pains had withered the grass in his yard. The little man of former times had become a fearsome apparition who no longer had any room in bed and slept on the floor, suffering more than could be imagined. He passed away the following Sunday, as divine service was being held in church.

Constantine Berca believed he was partly to blame, and he kept turning over in his mind whether this latest episode and the one with shepherd Andreiaş Gozgu from Sălişte were proof that he'd been born on this earth to throw things out of kilter rather than to help them settle into their groove. He did not go to the funeral, but on the day the body of Enache Mâzgău was laid to rest, he left the house that afternoon without Domnica seeing him or suspecting she wouldn't be seeing him for a long while. A single glance and she would've understood what doubt had overwhelmed his soul, and she would try to console him, fearing he was going to reckon with the fays for having chosen him, for binding his word to his deed. For where could those words have ended up in the deeps of the earth if not with those maidens who play game with the lives of men?

Constantine Berca first went to the orchard. Innkeeper Dulubaş saw him pass, then Ioan, the second son of Niculae Welldigger, who later would tell all those willing to listen what he saw, as he was the last to glimpse Berca's face before he left. No words could describe the pallor of his cheeks, or his air of abandonment on this unfamiliar and unfriendly earth. He was a man without refuge, wandering and lost.

Berca crossed the orchard and climbed toward the top of the hill, then up the Knoll, northward, to the wild woods. He stopped and wished to pray for forgiveness of his sins of anger, but he could not find the strength. The fir trees were swaying gently, caressed by the wing of an evening wind. The first stars began to shine in the region of the Big Dipper, and behind him the long snaking valley of Our Lady's River was plunged into shadow. He was unable to fasten his gaze on any one thing, as though each thing were so weightless that it melted and flowed away, eluding him. A deep sleep seemed to brush him softly, but he did not heed its voice, because he knew who was behind a sleep such as this. He searched the sky for the evening star, which, enveloped in cloud, heralded the dusk, and he prayed to it: he begged to be released from the spell of his words possessing too much power. The full moon, a golden imperial thaler, was also enveloped in cloud, denying Earth her light and erasing all roads of return. His steps were lost in the forest, in the deepest darkness. He let the path carry him where it willed. The branches lashed his face and scratched him, as if wishing to halt him in his tracks. The smell of cool, moist earth filled his lungs, intoxicating him with a sweet, heady perdition. After walking for a few moments, or for a few hours, looming into view before him was the portal with ebony carvings at the entrance to the cave, flanked, like a palace, with Venetian lamps and columns of encrusted wood, with thick, heavy chains and black bolts the girth of a man's trunk. He walked over the flagstones, which were as hot as the hob of a stove, and, reaching the steps that led into the depths, he began to descend without looking back. It was the first time he had come to that endless subterranean realm other than in sleep, just as the fays had prophesized. It had been fated that his body would reach the place where no men come other than in dream, and only when they are called, whether to be released from something or to learn a skill taught nowhere else. For the fays it was a game, but some men would lose their minds on such a journey. Constantine Berca stooped to avoid the stalactites of darkness that bristled from the roof of the cave like a forest, a roof so lofty one's gaze could not reach it, but where bats could be sensed flapping through the air. The walls were illumined by torches that gave off a stifling smoke and crackled as they were devoured by eternal flames, for their light was without beginning or end. Berca walked such a long way that he was gradually overcome by oblivion. It was longer than the road to Bucharest, longer than the road to Rahova. And he no longer knew who he was, from what country he came, or whither he went, because all that remained before his eyes was dream, transforming all, seeming to change him, too, into someone else for a second time. He emerged from the end of that secret way into a place of light, a place different from the palace he had seen in his dream, which he was now expecting to find once more, and he felt as rested as a babe after a peaceful and enchanted sleep, more at peace with himself than he had ever been. Yet he knew he hadn't slept even for an instant.

He now found himself on the top of a hill with ruddy earth, with huge rocks, so dry that not a single blade of grass sprouted toward the sky. The air was moist and hot, a salty odor. In the valley was a city with houses huddled one next to the other, white and covered in a crust of whitewash scorched and peeling in the sun. He also saw people with faces scorched by the sun, shod with wood soled sandals, and he saw their gendarmes, who were dressed strangely, he saw children playing and dark-eyed women, bakers scorching already dry bread in ovens, merchants exchanging various currencies, and when he later heard that the name of the city was Piraeus, he thought this a new trick played on him by the daughters of the Emperor of the Depths.

When he learned how far from home he was, having taken this path through the land of the endless subterranean reaches, Constantine Berca felt an overwhelming desire to return. He could find no trace of the way back as the hill had closed up unawares. He knew no Greek, and he did not have on his person any of those wonderful new documents the government had brought to Evil Vale. Berca went down to the seashore on the first evening and found shelter beneath some sun-scorched rocks.

At that same hour, Domnica sensed that her husband had wandered off and become lost, and the matter was more tangled than if he had merely lost his way on the mountain. She went to Old Woman Fira and persuaded her to read the future in the grains of wheat, or in the cards, or in the blades of grass, to discover what had become of her husband. Then from the very first signs given by the spell Old Woman Fira read:

"He is alive and well, but he cannot understand a single word of what is spoken around him, and the power of his words has been taken away from him, as he himself wished. The fays did not wish to receive him and they turned his steps toward another place in the world, whither they brought him by a secret path of one day's walking."

Turning the wheel of fortune once more and reading in the cards, she said:

"He left to pacify his heart, and now he wants to return, cleansed of anger. But the task is by no means easy and we must help him."

When Old Woman Fira tried to read the future in the grains of wheat, the matter took on a different complexion. By taking that hidden route, Constantine Berca had erased all trace of his leaving, and no spell could discover where he was, for on the visible surface of the earth he seemed not to have gone anywhere. The grains of wheat indicated that he was at home — as if he had not even left his own backyard. Nevertheless, the cards with their thirty-two faces felt his longing to return home straightaway from a foreign land.

The fact that he could no longer find the entrance to the cave that had led him to the ends of the earth was divined by Old Woman Fira as a great impediment that kept him bound to faraway places. And when the Bible fell open at a particular page near the end, she said:

"Let us cast a spell for the sake of the Acts of the Apostles and let us pray that he shall receive the gift of speaking in tongues, so that he will find his way home. He is going to need the gift of speaking Greek."

Perhaps this is how it happened that Constantine Berca learned Greek in a few short weeks, a few words, as much as was needed, and he began to work as a carpenter for the merchants of Piraeus. News of his great skill working wood spread and made him much sought-after in the port. Then he met Captain Christou Sava, who needed a hand for his ship bound for Constanța. The captain was from a sheep-breeding family and in his youth had herded flocks so large their edges stretched as far as the horizon. He had changed his trade because he was in love with the sea. He could only breathe, he said, above the waves. For him, the sea was bound-less and alive. It seemed to have called him, that it was always waiting for none other than him. He had served as a ship's hand in every capacity until after years of storms and long journeys he had risen to the position of captain, master of his own vessel. He was a man who made his own rules on ship. He had navigated over the years from Port Said to Gibraltar, borne onward by an unusual dis-quietude: he was at war with boundlessness. He had presentiments of storms and cyclones and knew, too, how to read the future — in the sea breezes and winds. This might be the reason why of all those who ever spoke with Constantine Berca he alone understood his estrangement, he alone believed him when he explained how he had come to Piraeus by no ordinary road, a hidden way through the mountains, a tunnel he could no longer find that passed close by the palace of the fays. Captain Sava listened to Berca tell his tale one sultry evening, after a day of exhausting toil, and finally he told him that he would not be tarrying much longer: they would soon raise anchor and set sail for Constanţa.

Once underway it became clear the captain had no need of a carpenter. He believed that dreams could reveal hidden treasure and new routes, thus it was well to have a dream-hunter on board on a long voyage. He considered the Wallachian carpenter such a hunter of dreams. He also knew that distance could arise from enormous sorrow, that death could be born from words, and that mountains have roots, like trees, but the sea has pages, countless, delicate pages, liquid pages heaped one on top of another. The captain knew the great power spells have in the world and that the ocean never dies. So this was how Constantine Berca set off for Constanţa, and he saw the islands of the Aegean Sea, the harmony of the waves and the winds that ripple together, islands as small as a farmyard and rocks as narrow as a mountain path, on which the sirens sit during storms. And he saw beneath the web of water red and green forms in which (so the captain told) the heroes of old used to divine their future and which are said to be stones endowed with life. Berca saw Holy Mount Athos from afar, streams of bluish, misty smoke rising from it to the heavens, the prayers of the monks, prayers in every color of the rainbow, just as they pray in every language on earth. As soon as Mount Athos disappeared over the horizon and the prayers were left in the ship's wake, Captain Sava once more began to deliver orders to his mariners, shouts mixed with oaths by all things holy, baptismal fonts and incense and devils and angels, as well as things too shameful to repeat, in all the languages of the Orient, an amalgam understood by none but him. On board were another four travelers the captain had agreed to take to Constanța, all of them having been gathered from around the port at the last moment: an Armenian trader of fine cloth and embroidery, a German student who had come to Greece in search of Homer, a Serbian monk from a monastery near Kiev, who was returning from Athens with some manuscripts, and a Greek tavern keeper who was moving his entire business from Piraeus to other parts. These men kept to themselves and did not mingle with the rowdy seamen; they came on deck only to see to their own affairs. After they passed the island of Samothrace, the wind died down and a torrid heat settled over the entire expanse of the sea. Then, one of the seamen discovered some damage and began to cry out in horror that the barrels of drinking water had burst.

Hearing the cry, the captain appeared on deck. What at first seemed a joke proved to be the most terrible ordeal the sea could cast at a man. At precisely that moment the wind died, and the ship remained motionless in the middle of the water with drooping sails, in a place where no land could be seen, rooted to the spot as if at anchor.

On seeing the disaster in the hold and in the sky, the captain outstretched his arms to the heavens and said: "The devil himself has done this!"

He could hardly believe his eyes. All the fresh water had indeed been lost, and nothing could be done about it. On the first day, they placed rags on the floor of the hold to soak up the film of fresh water left after the barrels had leaked. But the water vanished as though it had been boiled, turning to vapor before their very eyes. They tried to preserve the condensation, to collect it in stretched canvas and drink the droplets, like the fairies in children's tales drink the drops of dew on blades of grass in the early morning. But there was not enough water for the twelve men on the boat, and the wind had still not picked up.

The next day, the captain found a single bottle of wine, which provided barely a mouthful for each man. But the warm wine merely inflamed their thirst all the more instead of quenching it.

On the third day, the Armenian merchant saw some shadows flickering over the water and spoke to them, and they seemed to be calling him. He wanted to climb down into the ship's only dinghy and row off northward. The others just managed to prevent him from wandering off into the labyrinth of the sea.

On the fourth day, under a murderous sun, in a world without wind and on an old ship floating aimlessly on the sea, they all sensed their minds were going, and they were overwhelmed by a languor heavier than the deepest intoxication. The sun burned ever fiercer. They kept one of the sailors from slashing his wrists. He had been dreaming that his thirst would be quenched if only he could drink his own blood. The helmsman tried digging into the wood of the mast in the hope that water would appear. During all this time, the monk sat in a corner of the deck and prayed, heard by none of the others. No one on the ship seemed to pay him any mind. Toward evening, the captain shouted at him:

"We're not dead yet! Save your prayers until then!"

On the fifth day, the monk said:

"Fill a barrel with seawater!"

No one hastened to obey him, all took this as a fresh outbreak of madness. No help forthcoming, the monk filled the only barrel by himself, patiently and dutifully hauling up dozens of buckets of seawater. Then he knelt, his brow pressed to the hoops of the barrel, and prayed in a whisper. When evening came, and no one was paying him any attention, the monk told them:

"Partake of the water of life!"

They all approached in disbelief. The captain drank first, then cried out:

"This water is not salty!"

They drank their fill, then fell asleep on the spot, exhausted, while the Serbian monk, without having taken a drop, continued to kneel in whispered prayer for the wind to rise. And while they slept, the secret breezes of the Aegean Sea awoke and set to work filling the sails. The captain could not believe it. The sails of the ship were suddenly filled to bursting. So after that unprecedented adventure Captain Sava's ship was once again under sail. To Constantine Berca it seemed that someone from another realm had been holding him there in the middle of the sea to stop him from reaching home, and if it hadn't been for the prayers of that monk, the ship would never have budged.

"What prayer was that?" Great-grandfather Berca asked the Kiev-bound monk.

"I saw a dance of invisible beings, and I prayed that it should cease. I prayed that the ring dance should stop its whirl and whatever flowed thence into this realm should cease."

"What ring dance?" asked Constantine Berca. "What is this all about? What do they want from us?"

"I do not know," answered the monk. "I do not know what it

means and I do not know what they want. I only prayed for it to stop."

Our great-grandfather realized the monk could read dreams and unravel their meaning, and in this way he was able to release the ship from the grip of the sea.

So Great-grandfather Berca reached Constanța. After another day and night of travel he reached Bucharest, and then Evil Vale. Yet he still didn't know if the spell had been broken or if the fays were still playing their games with the places he walked.

The gate was closed at home, and Elifterie was sleeping curled up on some straw by the new stove Berca had finished making before he was overwhelmed by that great unrest of his youth and his strange journey to Athens. Domnica had been weaving a peculiar colorless cloth, which she unraveled at night. She was the first to embrace him, although she could barely recognize him with his beard and sunburnt face. She had understood that his failure to find peace of mind had flung him to faraway places, and she knew of the spell she'd sent to his aid.

"I know all men have their hour of recklessness and madness when they are capable of chasing shadows to the ends of the earth."

Constantine Berca replied:

"The shadows are no more. I won't be leaving again."

And with that nothing would ever seem to change the course of events in the village of Evil Vale in the middle of the mountains.

3

Before bedtime, I heard Miruna ask Mother if she knew that the beautiful city of Athens, the one with white houses and surrounded by rocks, was at the ends of the earth, beyond the place where the winds die, and if the captain of the Vlașca brigands, Oarță Aman, was still alive and still terrorizing travelers on the motorway. We had gone to Bucharest by car a few times and had seen that forest, rather what was still left of it. And it was not all that dark or terrifying.

Miruna now had many questions. She wanted to know the location of the entrance to the land of the endless subterranean reaches, and if it were true that by falling asleep only in certain places on the Knoll could you enter through a portal half-dream, half-real. Grandfather had all the answers. The portal was lost among the grass to the north, perhaps on the mountain, among the juniper bushes, perhaps on some crag. Or it might merely be a hole in the ground, or a shadow in the forest that never followed the course of the sun. But it could never be used as one willed, and Berca never returned to the palace in the tale.

"It's the strangest tale I've ever heard," said Miruna. "How could anything like that exist?"

"That tale is nothing compared to this," as Niculae Welldigger had said to Father Dimitrie in that distant time. "Now the village gossip is all about something else — the end of the world."

Our grandfather told us how back then the village was full of old folk who knew all sorts of ancient skills, fortunetelling and healing, blending the waters with the lives of men, curing the ills of the earth. Old Woman Fira was merely the oldest of all the spellworkers, and she had stopped spellworking because the priest had frightened her with the fires of hell. Now it was impossible to find out who had started the rumor about the Apocalypse. The priest thought the Lord wanted to drive us mad, and then all sorts of thoughts sprang up and dispersed. It might have been around the time New Year's Eve of 1900 was approaching when one Sunday evening, on a night of a full moon, a goddaughter of Old Woman Fira, known throughout the village as Baba Safta, claimed she had read in the cards that the end of the world was nigh.

"This lie of divination will be the old biddies' last," proclaimed Father Dimitrie, happy to have such an occasion to drive out superstition. "Now there'll be an end to all this nonsense, because reading cards and grains of wheat will prove to be wrong! Let them believe for a while. When it will turn out they were mistaken, only then will they see how deceitful fortunetelling is and how great the power of faith."

"It can't be the end of the world," announced Old Woman Fira at a séance a week later. "I haven't got wind of anything of the sort, not in the cards, not in the grains of wheat."

It was true. She kept trying to discern the future; she wouldn't let it elude her secret powers. Father Dimitrie was disappointed when he learned of it. She had been the only person he had converted and cleansed of the sins of witchcraft. After Old Woman Fira said that the end of the world was in fact not on its way, the two old women became implacable enemies.

"But what if she's right, and the Apocalypse is coming in 1900," Welldigger asked the priest during confession.

Welldigger also told Constantine Berca about the disturbances in the waters that lay in the depths of the mountain, which he could sense in the twitching of his enchanted twigs. But maybe the two weren't connected, maybe the year 1900 would not usher in the end of the world but a new king, or the year a new prophet is born, or a new empire founded.

It was then that Father Dimitrie's heart was overcome with doubt. He must have wondered if there wasn't some truth to all those spells. For one whole night he prayed, wracked between despair that all the heresies might be true and fear that the signs laid out in the Book of Revelations could now be read, signs he knew very well could always at least halfway reflect any given moment in time. It was not until after that night of prayer in the village's old wooden church that the priest heard a voice, and this voice commanded:

"In Evil Vale a church of stone and brick must be built next to the wooden one, a church that will last a thousand years."

This was the sign Father Dimitrie had been waiting for. So, the end of the world would not be coming in the next thousand years, and that was all he needed to know. In less than a year he managed to mobilize the entire village, having them work and live as if there had been no tales of the end of the world, as if the Creation had remained unfinished. He conducted the building work with the energy of a pharaoh supervising the construction of his own pyramid. Master builders arrived from Câmpulung, famed icon painters from Brașov. They brought a sanctified bell from the Metropolia: a fresh sound ascending the heavens among the bells of Christendom, as now befitted the tiny hamlet of Evil Vale. Let it be known far and wide that Good Tidings had at last reached this village and that Christianity was vanquishing the last remnants of pagan belief, just as Saint George once vanquished the dragon. Some thought the sole reason for haste was the priest's advanced age. He wanted to leave finished works behind him. Father Dimitrie, however, had clear sight, and each day his booming voice would tell them how the folks of Evil Vale would be summoned at the Last Judgment to be admonished for all their sins only to be forgiven those sins according to the measure of these walls. "And what walls have we built?" the priest would ask, pointing his finger to the sky. "A church of stone," some would reply. "Never mind that," the priest murmured, "that was carved from rock six hundred years ago." For a time Father Dimitrie had lived in proximity with the light, seeing what the angels see, nourishing himself with the bread of angels, which is to say, with the Holy Ghost. For as long as it took to build the church of brick not far from Învârtita Lake, his face was pallid, like wax, his cheeks grew hollow, and his hands made a rustling noise in the air, like wings. And when someone would ask how much longer it would take to build, he said, "Creation has not yet concluded!"

His transformation continued its course undisturbed until the day Old Woman Fira went to Father Dimitrie to beg him to officiate a Mass to anathematize Baba Safta because she'd been using her fortunetelling powers to prophesize the end of the world. The soothsaying battle between the two old women had become a political struggle between great experts in the field, and one of them was requesting the support of the Church, the impact of which was as abrupt as the Fall. Coming to as if after having fallen a long way to Earth, Father Dimitrie was horrified by her words. His countenance became human once more, and he exclaimed in the voice of a young man:

"No such service exists in the canons of the Church! What do you mean, a Mass of anathematization? The ancestral Church has no such rite!"

The heresy was all the graver the more Old Woman Fira was incapable of accepting that a fortuneteller addled by old age could not be anathematized, honestly and righteously, before the Lord and congregation, that she could not be cursed during Sunday Mass, to the music of the liturgy, between the sermon and the final Paternoster before communion. Father Dimitrie raised his hand to his heart. He was so astonished by her request that his heart was stricken with grief. For ten days he was afflicted and hovered between life and death. On the tenth day, he arose, went out to the porch, gazed to the heavens, and whispered:

"Has this woman really understood nothing at all?"

On the fifth day of his sickness, the news reached him that Old Woman Fira and Baba Safta had made peace and were now casting spells together in search of the truth about the impending Apocalypse. After long hours reading the future in the grains of wheat, deep into the night, they discovered nothing more than a slight decay in the world's equilibrium, as if a world were about to die, but one that was tiny, incomplete, and ungainly. They both came to the same conclusion, and they told it to the rest of the village: the future of the world was luminous, but the cattle were in great danger of remaining barren, the crops would be mildewed, in the coming winter the potatoes might rot in the earth, we would all die one by one, at intervals, and we could ask no more than this from the Heavenly Father.

The building of the church in Evil Vale lasted fourteen months, and by the time it was completed a human color had returned to Father Dimitrie's cheeks and the plums and the apples had ripened in the village orchards, the same as in any other year. The end of the world had not come. The prophecy was forgotten.

Father Dimitrie had been right to rejoice at first. After the vagaries of their fortunetelling, the old women's predictions had proved to be groundless. Not one of their auguries could be believed any longer. They had begun to try their fortunetelling hand at everything from marriages to trivial haggling, and the more attempts they made the heavier the baggage of their defeats became. Then something strange happened, a true adventure for the world of spellcasting and fortunetelling, which was not to be surpassed in Evil Vale until the advent of industrially manufactured coffee and a completely different system for reading the grounds. Old Woman Fira and Baba Safta, independently of one another, the one on the hill, the other in the vale, said:

"Soon the king himself will visit Evil Vale."

This happened in the years when King Carol would not have left his palace in Bucharest for anything in the world, so exasperated he was by what he knew he would invariably see on his travels: the unpaved roads and the unkempt streets full of carrion. This was why the fortunetellers' latest prediction was all the more unbelievable. This general disbelief continued until the Thursday when four boyar gigs brought German surveyors and Italian masons, who produced charts from their bags and began to measure the length and breadth of one of the meadows toward the mountain. They finally compared their notes and decided:

"This is the place."

The Evil Vale folks were left in boundless amazement on the morning when ten builders from Bucharest proceeded toward the mountain. The divination had come true:

"The king is building a palace in Evil Vale."

Back then, the whole world was afflicted with building fever, and the village was enriched with not just a new church but also houses, bakeries, stables, hardware stores, summer kitchens, and brandy stills, yet no one apart from the fortunetellers had ever suspected that those years would also bring the building of a royal palace right next to the village. It seemed to be true that the king had been impressed by the tale of this place overlooked by governmental regulations, and he wished to do something for the village he was to refer to in a speech as *the last virgin land in Europe*. The fact that the building work was not to be completed until thirty years later, under a different king, did not in any way tarnish the merit of the old soothsayers. Many times they had managed to beguile the vicissitudes of time and to issue true prophecies; even Father Dimitrie was obliged to admit it, one fine day at a wedding, after a glass of red wine:

"All these years those old women have been one word ahead of me even when they are mouthing the words of the liturgy."

For the old women, this was merely the beginning of a long line of birth announcements, weddings, and other mundane matters, without their erring overly much. Their prestige was as great as that of the Church and the gendarmes. This happened back when the priest could count more than thirty fortunetellers among the two thousand two hundred souls inhabiting the village — a veritable industry. When the tale reached this point, Miruna interrupted once more to ask:

"How much of all this is true, Grandpa?"

Grandfather even had a tale about the clouds, the sun, the mountain, the creation of the world, the Lord God, the wise hedgehog, the Emperor of the Clouds and his daughters with their trains of azure, but Miruna would never leave off what interested her. On a Saturday evening she asked:

"I want to see, Grandpa, I want to see all the things you've told me."

On the following Sunday, Grandfather took Miruna to church, where she met Old Woman Fira for the first time. And she beheld a woman older than time itself, her memory addled, her head slightly trembling, her eyes milky white. She saw Elifterie from the brandy still sleeping in the sun, in a state of boundless tranquility, and she heard the voice of Father Dimitrie, whose age Grandfather said much exceeded that of Methuselah. The priest told Miruna he was more than one hundred and ten years old. As they were walking along the road on the way home, hand in hand, Miruna launched into a new string of questions, all of which concerned time.

"Has it been a long time since you were a kid, Grandpa?"

Numbers are in fact of no use to anyone, because nothing ever changes. Evil Vale is always the same. The ages of man are not like the ages of trees, for they are not measured in the same way. Birds of prey do not live as long as hens, or wolves and bears as long as cats. Things cannot be gauged by the same measure. Time is different for each thing. And the fact that Old Woman Fira, Elifterie, and Father Dimitrie are still alive, just as aged as they were when Niculae Berca was a child, is merely a matter of dispensations from the laws of nature that allow time to be swathed like a shawl around certain people, a disturbance that is called deathless life, about which there is an old fairy tale where the most interesting character is not the scorpion or the woodpecker but Time itself.

4

During that summer holiday when we were told the story of the journey to Hellas, Miruna had a fever and her first nightmare. Our parents were not in Evil Vale at the time, and something happened that frightened her. It was the summer we learned that the encrusted face of Christ can be seen on a grain of wheat. A snake slithered onto the porch of the house. Miruna grabbed Grandmother's spindle, the only thing at hand, and stood stock-still, at a loss of what to do. And that was how Grandfather found her, silently looking the serpent in the eye.

It was nothing more than a common house snake. At first Grandfather did think it might be a black viper, which can poison even giants, but he realized it was a house snake, so he clapped his hands in a way that was very loud, and the snake knew who was master of the house and slithered away. It found a hole in the ground outside by the steps, and therein it vanished.

By that evening, Miruna had become feverish, and overnight she fell gravely ill. Grandmother understood that the snake had cast a spell on her. Miruna shivered the whole night long, and the next day she told us she had dreamed of snakes. Her eyes ached, as if she had been gazing at a strong light for a long time. Grandmother made her an infusion of herbs she had gathered and did not close her eyes for one moment. Nor was it an easy night for Grandfather. All the things that had ever disquieted him gathered together to greet that strange fever. In fact, he was fearful his tales were causing her nightmares. I recall that Miruna was talking in her sleep about the head of a dragon . . .

In truth, that summer I thought about whether life sometimes settles into such a groove that things take on the most tragic of all possible aspects, and I began to suspect that children's storytellers are part of an adult conspiracy, that they tell their stories in such a way that they bear little resemblance to life, concealing the real endings, changing them into happy endings, like in "Snow White." It is only much later that children open their eyes to the world and gain an image of the whole. Grandfather did not seem to be part of the conspiracy. He let slip a lot of stories that didn't have a lullaby ending. And, too, there was a story about the things he refused to tell us. It is said that the one who controls the ending of stories is a creature with a body made of mist, with eyes of azure and wings of night. Grandfather called him the Angel of the Story. And it is this angel who decides when this or that child is to be shown how things really are, before they become adults.

At dawn, when Miruna opened her eyes, as if nothing had happened, she saw Grandfather leaning over her, frowning, with the expression on his face that sometimes used to scare people. She frowned, too, and asked him:

"What happened, Grandpa?"

His face brightened. He clasped her in his arms and laughed. Then Miruna asked:

"Is it true that while I was asleep you spoke with a creature made of mist and smoke?"

Grandfather then began to look at Miruna with different eyes. He now had confirmation: she could read dreams, whereas I, he told me, could not read anything, not even faces.

Niculae Berca experienced days truly more terrible than those that followed after our parents, Miruna and I in tow, left Evil Vale. And not just because he didn't like to be alone, as he was never really alone: he had Grandmother, he had other grandchildren. It was something else. We were the ones he'd chosen to receive his stories. He had shown Miruna and me the small, chilly room where he had been schooled, he had shown us the orchards, the land we had received — the whole of our line — because Great-grandfather had fought the Turks at Rahova, he had shown us the whole village, with all its legends, and it was only then that things began to cohere. For us it was a beautiful story, one that told us who we are. Otherwise, when alone he would go into the garden, where the only thing to be heard was the unruffled silence of the mountain, and it was as if he could see for real one of those tales he now told to his grandchildren, but whose main character was himself, in a different guise, child or youth, grown man — a story that was no weightier than a will-o'-the-wisp, as if a thread of spider silk held it suspended in the upper air, because it is no more, having long been left behind. Having transformed the world that no longer existed into the world of fairy tales, he could not remain unchanged. Of the village folk from past days, those who dug wells following an ancient craft, or who walked without fear and unarmed among the beasts of the forest, guarded by spells, of all the faces of long ago, all that remained was a tale no less fantastic than that of Our Lady of the Rocks or Aleodorus the Emperor. Sitting alone on the grass, Niculae Berca remembered the springs of his childhood, when his mother would paint the motif of a spiraling labyrinth on Easter eggs, a pattern long forgotten today. He saw winters with bands of masked revelers, and those endless games and inventions that all children used to play. He saw the first storybook he ever opened, which many years later fell dog-eared from his hands when he began to read the newspapers, a book that told of Caliph Harun-al-Rashid and flying carpets, creatures with magical powers shut up in bottles, astrological armillary spheres, merely a glancing touch of which would be enough to plunge you into eternal oblivion, knights in enchanted armor, talking animals, and beasts that could see through stone. His world of fairy stories, a world of distant childhood, would forever represent to him the closest earthly image of heaven. Grandfather told us that each person sooner or later comes to see the world with the eyes of the fairy stories heard in childhood, that our soul moves along the string of meanings and wonders we hear during our faraway first age of life, and that afterward the whole world is structured according to their pattern. Thus Niculae Berca set off into the world a very long time ago, and thus he survived the two world wars so he could tell us tales of times long passed.

When we returned with our parents to Evil Vale, he was overjoyed he would be able to continue. What he told us now was not about our great-grandfather, his father, but about himself. I well remember the first of those tales. It was about his first trip to Bucharest, when he went with his father to the merchants of the Obor Market. On the way, he passed through a number of big towns, through villages nestling among vine-laden hills, then through the villages of the plain, where you could see wattle and daub huts next to the stone houses of the wealthier peasants. As they passed through the Vlăsiei Forest on the way to Bucharest, Constantine Berca told him about the place:

"Look, these are the woods of Oarță Aman the bandit."

It was no longer the deep forest of yore, for they had already begun to cut it down to make way for the railways fanning from Bucharest in all directions. The woods had begun to thin out.

The next day, after they had finished their business at the Obor Market, Niculae Berca could sense his father's high spirits. His father came to him smiling and said:

"Today we are going to ride on the tram, like gentlemen."

You might not know what the tram was like in those days. It was a wonder greater than the train. It rumbled along on its tracks past houses, down narrow winding streets, its hinges creaking at every corner. Niculae saw the whole of Moșilor Avenue, as far as the Dâmbovița River, and then the streets leading to Victory Avenue, the ones on the way to the Royal Palace. These were streets of two- and three-story buildings, and they were surrounded by flower gardens, with fences of iron railings, not wooden planks, which were painted black or green and had wrought-iron flowers and birds. There were also restaurants with terraces and outdoor tables adjacent to the street, always thronged with people, where porters carrying sacks and dairymaids with large pails continually passed, where insolent, surly coachmen drove their horses, and busy gentlemen wearing monocles and ladies with feathered hats and trailing gowns could be seen inside coaches. He would never forget this image of Bucharest.

Old Niculae Berca was now strolling along the worn path

through the garden, which led faraway, up to the Knoll. He felt dizzy. This had been happening to him a lot lately. Fleeting images jumbled together in his mind. He had to sit down on the dry earth. I saw his face become altered, his hand raise to his chest. The purling of the brook. The sky, boundless sky, not a shadow of a cloud. A beautiful autumn, a late autumn. After a few moments, he smiled and told us it was nothing more than a momentary fatigue. He told us later that he had remembered the story of Gheorghe Vartolomeu, which he recounted to us by the fireside during the Christmas holidays when our parents left us at Evil Vale once more. I remember that when he told us the story, our cousin Matei was also there with us. Grandfather managed to prod our minds as well as frighten us, for this tale was true from start to finish.

In the middle of the forest, on the western slope, there was a wide glade where the folks of old wanted to build a cabin. You can still see the ruins of that undertaking today, the toppled walls of burnt wood eroded by the rain. The inside of the structure would be covered in hoarfrost in autumn, and the she-wolves hid their cubs there in spring. It was overgrown with weeds. But before that, three young shepherds had agreed to form a partnership and to merge their flocks so as to share their labors in summer, when after the feast of Ss. Constantine and Elena they took their sheep up into the mountain pastures, and in winter, when they led them back down into the Plain of Teleorman. The spot where they intended to build their sheepfold was virgin forest, where none dared to tread, let alone build a structure, so dark and inimical it was. And Old Woman Fira had in fact told the three lads not even to set foot in that forest as it had been said since time immemorial that it was enchanted, that those woods stood above the very palace of the fays, which lies buried in the depths, two versts below Evil Vale. But Gheorghe Vartolomeu, who was young and never one to be turned back once he had set his mind to something, told Old Woman Fira:

"Magic spells don't frighten us!"

Old Woman Fira explained it to them nicely, but she could not change their minds, although she told them many things, even this:

"The mountain is boundless. Choose a place for yourselves anywhere you will, just not in that glade!"

It was simply a matter of how the world is divvied up: that part of the forest was not for humans. Unlike their parents, the young folk of Evil Vale no longer respected the lands where no man should tread.

The very next day the lads began to cut down the oaks, to join the timber in the way people built back then, without using nails or anything else made of iron. Then they spent their first night in the glade, one keeping watch by the fire while the others slept, until dawn. The morning seemed to them the most beautiful they had ever seen. It seemed they had nothing to fear any longer for they had taken mastery of the place, and the words of the old women had seemingly dissolved in the winds, for the sun now shone upon the foundations of their new dwelling. Myriad beads of dew glistened like eyes all around them. Then they gazed down from the mountain, through the trees, and in the valley they saw the village spread out, with its barns and houses scattered here and there. They fell in love with that place, inexorably, and they had no mind to descend into Evil Vale ever again. Once the sheepfold was ready, the first to keep watch there with the sheep overnight was Gheorghe Vartolomeu, who seemed born for a hermit's life in the forest. It was a tranquil, honeyed night, one of those nights that bewitches sleep and bears it away into deep, unknown places. But Gheorghe Vartolomeu awoke after midnight, because the silence had been quenched in the murmur of purling waters, like a gushing spring. He arose to the strains of a confused and indecipherable hymn whose music drowned out the sound of children's laughter. He rose to his feet and listened to the hymn. It was like a choir of young voices in church, as though within an invisible altar. Going outside, he saw them for himself. They were dancing in a ring a hand's breadth above the ground, their bodies illumined from within. He stood motionless for a long while — he, too, had heard the legend of the fays and knew that he who moved when hearing their song would be forever stooped. They were the mistresses of the oak wood, creatures of sap, love, and vapor, living eternally and playing with mortals when they snared them in their power. Gheorghe Vartolomeu saw all twelve of them, some with fair hair, others with dark hair, hair so long it reached to the ground. His eyes fell on one of them in particular, one with blue eyes and hair as black as a raven, garbed in a gown of pure azure with Levantine patterns. She sensed him. Aware that some- one was staring at her, she broke away from the ring dance and, like all spirits that beguilingly answer the summons of the heart, came smiling toward Gheorghe Vartolomeu, gazing into his eyes and dancing close to him. He tried to make the sign of the cross, but his arms were bound as though in tight straps, and he could not budge an inch. Her steps were different than those of mortals, half-walking, half-dancing, a hand's breadth above the grass, and her bare shoulders, which he saw the better as she approached, looked like sculpted marble. The ground around her was garbed in a soothing glow, like the light of day. She opened the door of the hut and went inside. She walked through the embers of the hearth without being burned, painlessly befriending the red-hot coals. And thence rose a red whirlwind of spark-filled air that enveloped him, enveloped the whole room.

Then she showed him the sheepfold transformed into a palace of porphyry and bedecked in precious stones, covered in carpets from southern lands:

"Do you wish this to be our house?"

But Gheorghe made no reply. This temptation was the hardest trial he had ever heard tell. She continued, untroubled by his silence:

"We shall live here together, the two of us, and our love will shine throughout the world like the sun."

She was so beautiful he wanted to cry out, "Yes!" But his strength of mind held him back. He knew this was a bewitchment, that all they said about the fays was true, and now he saw the games they played with humans.

While her sisters in the glade danced slowly, chanting a spell in a tongue unknown to mortals, the ethereal temptress bent down to Gheorghe Vartolomeu and embraced him. The blood pounded his cheeks as her touch devoured him and placed mad desire in his heart.

"Or better still," she went on, "come with me into the land of pine needles, and we shall live there in endless love."

Gheorghe Vartolomeu gathered the last of his strength and pushed her away, and not saying a word, he closed his eyes. He'd been impelled to move by her touch, burning him, by her breath, unhinging his mind. Unable to resist, he had moved, when the only defense would have been to remain motionless. Then, all of a sudden, their chanting and their ring dance ceased.

The next morning, when his two friends returned to the hut in the enchanted glade, they heard the heart-rending lament of a distant flute. It was the earthly image of an immense longing, a peerless longing, the heart's yearning for a faraway land, one for which no human words exist, only music. They saw him sitting there, eyes vacant, playing music such as they'd never heard before.

"What's with you?" they asked him.

The fire had gone out, and he had no other answer than that lament. He lacked something he knew he would never again possess. He knew he would never again see what he had seen that night. They were unable to make him tell what he felt, not even when the old women performed a counter-spell on him, not even when Father Dimitrie read to him and prayed at his bedside the whole night through. Gheorghe Vartolomeu had lost the power of speech. Interposed between him and other men was now the music of lament, an endless series of doors, all locked with the notes of a flute. In his song there was nothing but shadows, smoke, and love. Listening to it, folks understood that the Vale of Tears was real, that such a place existed on earth, that someone had been there and returned with a grief they could barely comprehend. His face had changed so much that everyone forgot his name, and for a while they called him Elifterie, many years before my grandfather, Niculae Berca, first met him in his distant childhood. As a matter of fact, in that world faces changed very little, while the names remained the same, as if endless files of people came into the world only to continue a role, a particle of what made Evil Vale what it was on this earth.

One winter evening, we went to see how Old Woman Fira read the future. We were with Grandmother. She had lit the old lamp in her room, its glow a waxen yellow. She whispered a charm, queer words we could not fathom, although some of them sounded like Romanian. Old Woman Fira was sitting with her eyes closed, in that light that had wandered in from ancient times, and she seemed to see far into the distance. The shadows flickered over the walls, and the hangings were transformed into huge horses about to bolt. I pressed against Miruna, and she put her arms around me. We were afraid. It was the first time we had heard that arcane language. The enchanted grains of wheat lay to her right, while the spell lingered nearby. The wheel of time began to turn, the bobbin spun, revealing and concealing. A journey came into view, she told Grandmother, a journey far away, over sea and over land. Someone was to set off into the world, said Old Woman Fira, now or next week.

"I'm going to Argeş next Sunday to market," said Grandmother.

But that seemingly foreign voice began to speak of something else, something other than what Grandmother had asked, and it told of what was written in the grains of wheat, and the grains told of Miruna's sons' sons, of languages we did not understand, of a land far from here, bounded by waters to the west and to the east. The bobbin spun, the lamplight emanating from the mirror dimmed, there was a scent of lamp oil, and the shadows revealed their secrets. Others would change their names, and in Evil Vale nothing would remain, except a graveyard with tumbled crosses over which tall grass would grow, and our stories would be forgotten, and our names would be forgotten. Only the fays would be left to emerge in the glade, but they would no longer find anyone on the mountain.

"What language is this, Grandma?"

"The charms are in Serbian and Slavonic. We don't know what they mean any more, but the words are still powerful, they still do their work."

Outside, beyond the yard, a stray dog was barking. The cold wind gathered from the Knoll the moist smell of the rain-soaked soil and the wind whistled in the treetops, summoning the clouds to cast their mantle over the stars. And the firmament seemed to shine with the prophetic grains of wheat rather than the eternal celestial bodies. At least that is how it appeared to me. Then Miruna started to cry. Grandmother took her in her arms, and we fled homeward. I was sorry we hadn't stayed to listen. Now I have begun somewhat to understand the unknown tongue with which Old Woman Fira mixed her words, and if I had stayed to hear the prophecy I would have read the future as if it were an open book, because that ancient tongue in which she cast her spells is intelligible if you close your eyes, breathe deeply, and spread wide your wings.

5

Grandfather's illness came after the second summer of storytelling. He lay in bed from dawn to dusk, beleaguered by a weariness and weakness beyond mere old age. When he allowed us to enter his room, we saw him in his unbuttoned white shirt, his chest bare, something unheard-of for him in the middle of the day. His hair disheveled, face drawn, the room seemed in disarray. I wanted to hold Mother's hand, but she was not there. I forgot that Miruna was there, even though she was standing beside me. The only thing I remember about that moment now, more than twenty years later, is that certain events unfold in such a way that you comprehend nothing at the time you're experiencing them. I was as blind as a mole and felt alone, and I saw that Grandfather was ill and his room was in disarray.

When we had been alone with him for just a few moments, I saw Miruna climb into his bed, stretch out beside him, and say:

"Grandpa, tell us another story . . ."

It was probably a joke. I saw Grandfather smile. He had difficulty breathing. Grandmother cleared away his food and waited for us to leave the room. But taking the game seriously, Grandfather asked Miruna in a whisper what kind of tale she would like to hear. She said she already knew the story of the famous Captain Christou Sava, who died at sea during a storm in the embrace of the sirens he had dreamed of his whole life long, and she did not want to hear the story of the brave Greuceanu again, a tale she knew very well, a classic in fact, or Ion Creangă's story "White Arab," which was now available on long-playing vinyl disc, or that of the heroic Muscel regiment that was decimated at Rahova, then at Turtucaia, and then at Odessa, in three different wars. Nor did she want to hear again the tale of Vlad the Impaler and his cruel justice, nor the story of the miracle-working Saint Filofteia, who sleeps for all eternity beneath Argeş Monastery. She did not want any of those tales. Miruna knew them all.

Grandfather closed his eyes, trying to bring to mind something else. And when he gazed once more around the room, his eyes settled on Grandmother's dowry chest, on which was depicted the crossing of the Danube in 1877 and the reunification celebrations of 1918. He remembered the time he went off to the front at barely twenty-one years of age. So Grandfather told us a tale that day, and even now I don't know how much of it was true and how much was fable.

Miruna gazed at Grandfather's face and listened. Every so often her fingers toyed with the tassels of the quilt. At the head of the bed was Grandfather's sheepskin jerkin with its unmistakable smell of walnut shells, not yet having imbibed the odor of medicaments. I was sitting at his bedside on a three-legged stool, my head resting on his hand, and he was speaking. Grandmother was waiting, and for a moment, just a moment, time seemed to stand still only for us.

When war broke out in Transylvania, said Grandfather, the news arrived in Evil Vale as usual, after a delay of a few days. The front was rumored to be along the Jiu River, following the heavy fighting over the mountain, in Câmpulung Muscel. Then news came that the front was along the Olt River, and fear shrank our hearts to the size of a flea, because it was accompanied by the news of a general mobilization in the mountain villages. Then the front moved even closer: along the Argeș River. And then no more newspapers of any kind came, and the village was left cut off, connected only to the four winds and the heavens. Until one fine day two sergeants with a corporal and seven privates showed up in Evil Vale, all of them fair-haired and exceedingly tall, bringing with them orders to requisition animals and corn. They spoke among themselves in a kind of broken Slavonic, although they wore the uniform of the German Army and were representatives of Imperial Germany here in the Făgăraș Mountains. They were no more than the advance guard of the German occupying forces, which had temporarily set up its headquarters in a boyar manor house near Domnești, a house clad in vines, with a carved wooden porch, on which they had hoisted the German and the Austro-Hungarian flags. Every evening, Colonel von Ziese would go onto the porch to watch the sun set and to gaze in horror upon that foreign and chaotic world where war had brought him and had now placed in his charge. Three weeks later the news came that the Germans had taken Bucharest. In the valley of Our Lady's River things settled into their new groove. In every village, gendarmes were replaced by German soldiers with orders to round up sheep, with or without lambs, and to take away butter and sacks of corn. For the first time the folks of Evil Vale saw typewriters, lamps powered by electric pile cells, coffee filters, packets of chocolate, tins of beans that could be opened using a kind of Z-shaped knife, and all kinds of other things from Germany not to be found in these mountains. German rule lasted only a year, but a number of stories have remained from that time. Many things took place during that year of the occupation, but it wasn't until a mounted patrol escorting an Austro-Hungarian courier vanished on a stormy night without trace that complications arose. Constantine Berca heard from Niculae Welldigger that the riders had gotten lost as they were hurrying through the mountains toward Transylvania, and at the spot locals called the Watershed they came upon a shepherd who helped them by showing them the way to the chasms. Three days later a major arrived with orders to investigate the mysterious disappearance of the courier and his escort as it seemed he'd been carrying a top-secret message for the Imperial Army. Where had they been seen last? Near the crags? Near the chasms? There was no trace of them anywhere. It had been so dark that not even the night itself saw anything — the major learned nothing. To make matters worse, their mapmakers had no precise charts of the labyrinth of deep forest paths winding near the chasm's edge, and the forays made by search parties on the ground had turned up nothing. Constantine Berca saw no great mystery in the disappearance, and he could clear it up straightaway: there was always a shepherd passing with his flock who could see everything that happened up on the mountain. The flocks did not wander over the mountain as they pleased, and a group of mounted soldiers couldn't go unobserved by the shepherds who took the same road as them. Colonel von Ziese did not know this. To him, the movements of the flocks and the shepherds seemed chaotic, lacking any order, and for the time being this impeded the progress of the investigation. To the eyes of the uninitiated, those villages might have seemed just as chaotic and disorderly as an oriental bazaar. A deeper understanding was needed. Thus the colonel got the idea to inquire throughout the village of each individual inhabitant what he thought had taken place on that stormy night. A general interrogation. The man who angered the colonel was Mihai, the son of Niculae Welldigger, who suggested to his interrogator that a group of young, armed men would have wanted nothing more than just to go back home.

"There is no desertion from the German Army!" roared Colonel von Ziese when the translator had relayed the answer.

Mihai Welldigger knew much better than him how things stood. After all, in his outhouse a fair-haired, Czech-speaking soldier would remain hidden until war's end, and no one discovered a thing as long as the price was a man's life.

Then came Constantine Berca's turn to be interrogated. In the meantime, he had gone to the attic with Mihai Welldigger, who knew how to read, and brought down all the newspapers he had received by subscription over the last thirty years, which his son had read to him every evening. They sat up until dawn collecting all the articles concerning the crimes perpetrated by Oarță Aman and his gang, the bandits led by Gheorghe Ologu and Radu Vedeanul from Pitești, murders on the highway in broad daylight, mail-coach robberies, and attacks on gendarme posts, everything that in the eyes of a foreigner with no understanding of the flow of time in Muntenia might be passed off as current. With these articles in hand, Berca went to Colonel von Ziese that morning when his turn came, and he submitted a formal complaint, which the commandant registered on the spot, against said Oarță Aman, whose banditry had now begun to impinge upon the communications of the German Army.

"But he's been dead for years!" said Colonel von Ziese's translator in Romanian.

"It's not true he's dead!" said Constantine Berca. "He's alive and commits robberies on the mountain, among the shepherds, leading the life of a bandit even after his gang was broken up when the gendarmes surrounded them."

Colonel von Ziese asked that every word of the old peasant be translated, then he demanded translations of each of the sensational news articles of twenty years earlier that Berca had produced. The more he heard about these events, the more his face darkened, and finally, shocked by such accounts, he nodded his head and said:

"Wallachia is a land of bandits!"

He realized additional troops would be required.

Old Woman Fira later was to discover via a spell to read the past that von Ziese had been a functionary in civilian life, an accountant or an inspector, but his family had once been wealthy in former days. The man had nothing in common with the army except a series of promotions during three years of war. He had not spent one day at the front, and the horror stories gleaned from the newspapers had a profound effect on him. Wanted posters appeared within a week on the lanes of the village offering a substantial reward for the head of one Oarță Aman, of whose existence the commandant now had no doubt. The fact that no one ever supplied any information was interpreted by the German authorities as the surest indicator that the bandit was still alive, was hunting down imperial couriers, and was being sheltered by the hostile populace of the area.

After a few weeks, Colonel von Ziese was on the brink of despair: all his measures to capture Oarță Aman had come to nothing, and his superiors were demanding immediate results. He decided to double the number of sentinels, to print fresh wanted posters offering an even larger reward, to lay ambushes using fake imperial couriers, and to organize lightning raids in all the places where the perfidious bandit might be hiding. Soon after the posters had been pasted onto the village fences, walls, town hall, churches, bridges, and wherever folks passed, a German soldier was ambushed by the outhouse of the very boyar manor where the area commandant himself was quartered. He was dragged inside, bound hand and foot, and beaten. Then Oarță Aman, who to the soldier seemed to have the consistency of shadow and an arm of iron, carved the sign of the cross on his cheek with a dagger. He spared his life and left him there, terrified and ashamed. Aman was then seen strolling down the village lane in broad daylight, his hands clasped behind his back like a gentleman of leisure. The wind blew through his body. Recognizing him from the picture on the wanted posters, which had been copied by hand from the only image available to the gendarmes, a blurred photograph taken immediately after the war against the Turks, the peasant women fled in terror. He resembled a man come back from the dead, his face decayed and dirty, the hollow sockets of his eyes glowing, his skeletal hands poking out of the sleeves of his cloak. The light of the sun shone right through his translucent frame, as insubstantial as a gust of wind. He laughed:

"Why so frightened? Didn't you pray for me to return, didn't you summon me to come and trample the Germans? Why are you so upset about it now?"

The German soldier with the slashed face reported he'd been cut with a barber's razor, and his superiors were all too eager to believe him. But the next day another German soldier turned up, having been slashed even more nastily, with three holy crosses carved into his cheek, all of a suspect symmetry. And then another, and then another, until the hallowed autumn Sunday when a yelling horseman came riding down the village lane on a black stallion, two daggers tucked in his waistband and a Vlaşca-style jerkin flung across his shoulders. It was the captain of the bandits himself, Oarță Aman, come back from the dead in the clear light of day, afraid of neither sun nor mortal men, fearing nothing, like a living man, dark of gaze and swift of movement. He passed the church at a gallop, without making the sign of the cross, and the bells began to chime on their own, swayed by the wind that had whipped up out of nowhere. Reaching the door of the command post, he pointed his finger at the Germans' rooms and roared, louder than his neighing horse:

"You will suffer something worse than death!"

His words left his mouth in Romanian and struck the windows of the old boyar manor in German. A violet wind had risen around him, whipping up dust from the road and leaves from the ditches. Then the villagers understood why Oarță Aman had not killed the German soldiers, because in war it is not the death of your enemy that counts, but his humiliation before you and before himself. He made them lie in hiding, cower and lose heart, this was his battle. It was for this he'd come from the world beyond. It sometimes happens in war that the dead themselves join the fray, yet the humiliated are forever banished from the ranks of the triumphant.

The village folk thus witnessed the dismissal of Colonel von Ziese by order of the High Commander, which village gossip got wind of as soon as the orders arrived, spreading the news of the dismissal all along Our Lady's River, a dismissal undoubtedly connected to that ill-omened day when, in his bedroom, Colonel von Ziese had used his own razor to carve into his cheek seven crosses in the form of Ursa Minor with a bloody Pole Star on his brow. Yet everyone knew he had in truth been the victim of the bloodthirsty Oarță Aman, who had been brave enough to enter the colonel's house, capture and slash him — a shadow that collared the colonel by entering through the wall and leaving through the mirror.

The enchanted virtues of the places in Evil Vale, which is said to lie above the castle of the fays, places where very curious apparitions and disappearances occur, only revealed themselves five years after the episode of Oarță Aman and Colonel von Ziese. The war had ended and the German Army had left. Niculae Berca returned home, and there followed the best years in our grandfather's life. He had never told us anything about those years. That summer, near the mountain, beyond the spot where His Royal Majesty had intended to build himself a hunting lodge, the shepherds met Professor Ambrozie one fine Wednesday. He was a most peculiar man, who tapped at the rocks of the mountain with tools somewhat resembling those of a mason. He strolled through the forest amid the bushes and weeds, digging up the earth with a soldier's spade. He clambered up the cliffs and dislodged boulders, numerous times nearly losing his footing. When he had an audience, however small, wherever he was on the mountain, he would begin to tell them stories of times long passed. He had arrived in a car that spluttered and smoked when the motor started up. The professor was lodged at the old inn of Constantine Dulubaş. He smoked a pipe filled with aromatic tobacco and wore a gilded monocle on his left eye, attached by a length of white silk instead of a chain. One evening, a few of the villagers gathered at the inn to hear his stories. One of them was Constantine Berca. The innkeeper, too, after pouring him a glass, sat down to listen. The professor told stories with an oratorical flair such as no one in Evil Vale had ever heard before and which left none unmoved.

"Your village was founded in 1335, after the Battle of Posada, when the King of Hungary filled his mouth with magic sand and made himself invisible in the thick of the fighting to escape with his life from the rain of rocks and vipers his foes were casting down on him from the top of the mountain."

The village folks laughed, as at a good joke. And this was only the beginning, as theories about the historical site of Posada were subsequently to materialize before their very eyes. Ambrozie conjured up a caricature of historian Nicolae Iorga, with his bushy beard and Goliath-like stature, then he invoked kings, chroniclers, and saints as his story required, introducing each to his audience with their own hidden vices or bad habits, all of which were familiar to the professor. Immediately after the Battle of Posada, he said, a handful of warriors received from the hand of Basarab the Great himself a golden bull entitling them to rule Evil Vale. They came here with their women, children, and flocks. By the early 1700s, the inhabitants numbered almost a thousand souls. Then in the 1860s, after the reforms under Cuza, the number doubled.

The professor bewildered the villagers with the figures and dates he juggled. And then he launched into his own theory, namely that Posada was slightly to the north of the village, past Învârtita Lake, which did not exist back then. That evening the villagers were good friends with Professor Ambrozie, until the moment he suggested, making the argument as clear as clear could be, that in his scholarly opinion they might consider changing the name of their village from Evil Vale to Posada. Some of the folks grew irate, and they told him these were good years for the orchards and it was not right to make light of a lucky name, one consecrated for such a long time in the holy church. Father Dimitrie had prayed two centuries for this name. The name could not be changed.

"You really believe that Evil Vale is a lucky name?" laughed Professor Ambrozie.

He then began a new spiral of tales, polemics, arguments, and gestures, whereby he explained that golden bulls from distant times placed Posada beneath Green Knoll, where the course of Our Lady's River narrows between the crags of Russian's Chasm downstream, where the road to Transylvania opens up for shepherds and their flocks. In his mind, this was clearly the spot where Posada had existed. The villagers, however, suspected (without telling anyone else) that this was where the third portal to the endless subterranean reaches lay. Given that everything the village knew was turned upside down by the professor's stories, innkeeper Dulubaș and a few others clapped his hat on his head, bundled him out of the inn and into his car, and showed him the way back to Bucharest. The professor rolled down the window and as his final argument invoked the secret blazon of the Basarab dynasty, the shield of the initiated knights, a coat of arms that proved his theory beyond any doubt: an angel seated above the crags of a bottomless valley, above which rose a tall cross. Pointing his finger to the heavens, he told them:

"I am a martyr on the altar of science!"

Then through the open window of his car the professor told them about the Basarab dynasty. He shouted that he had discovered the key to unlocking the secret of that dynasty of Cuman princes and the motto inscribed on their secret blazon: *Prolem sine matre creatam*. No sooner had he shouted these words — as if he had recited a magical formula — than he was engulfed by a whirlwind, motorcar and all, leaving in its wake the stench of burnt gasoline, tinder, brimstone, and the final defeat of his theory by the far more convincing theory of Professor Iorga, who posited that Posada was situated ten kilometers to the east.

"Did you see the way he vanished?" said the innkeeper, "he was the Unclean One himself!"

Since that time village lore has included the tale of how the devil himself came to Evil Vale and tried to change its consecrated name to something entirely unsuitable.

Grandfather's story came to an end. Evening had come, and with it, sleep.

The next day, too, he told us a story, which he recalled when he opened his eyes and saw once more the one-hundred-year-old Swiss pendulum clock he had inherited from his father, the only wildly extravagant purchase anyone in our family had ever made. Apparitions silently danced around it, and rather than a story, something else caught his eye, the real image of State Security troops coming to Evil Vale almost thirty years earlier to scour the mountain paths where Colonel von Ziese had once hunted shadows. There were four grim-faced battalions in all. Those were the days when one could hear stray gunshots at night, fired from new Russian automatic rifles. They were on the trail of anticommunist partisans hiding in the mountains. "The Americans are coming," Old Man Manole Dridu used to whisper, his ear pressed to the radio set. He was remembering the old man's face and how it winked merrily. "The Americans are coming," is all he would say. And Father Dimitrie, then more than two hundred years old, prayed, forgoing sleep, forgoing food, prayed that the Americans would come, that he would be able to repair the belfry and then to make a donation to Râmeț Monastery and to make a pilgrimage to Mount Athos, and then to Jerusalem, for Creation had not yet come to a close. "These are the seven trumpets!" said the priest, who could no longer hear what was said to him but heard very well the bells of heaven. "I can no longer tell the future," said Old Woman Fira, who was going blind. "For as long as they are here, in the village, the grains have no power. The future is tied up in knots." When it is scoured, the forest grows even darker and closes its portals to the hidden realm, and this is why when the soldiers discovered the nest of the last unicorn, with its scent of rosewater and teardrops, the woods tangled their paths, from the Knoll into the distance, as far as Nehoiu, and caused them to hear chimerical voices, throwing the platoons into confusion and proving that no soldier can obey orders if harried by unseen creatures, which might be beautiful young women dancing, or towering beasts, or bandits from a bygone era dashing headless across the rocky slopes. A team of military cartographers led by a lieutenant were then given the mission to draw up a complete chart of the forest so that no one would ever be able to hide out there again. They went in circles for days on end, managing only to draw labyrinths of chlorophyll, green maps without ingress or egress, interlocking bands, funnels, tunnels, like ferns twisting around an oak, like a clew knotted around the Knoll, around the village of Evil Vale. Niculae Berca saw their anger and misfortune, and in his sleep he smiled, for this was not the real map, as he well knew. Then he heard the voice of a young woman, whispering something to him in an ancient tongue, as if she were reading from a golden bull, and only then did he fall asleep once more, and it seemed to him that nothing of any of this remained. That tale was to stay unfinished, and Miruna and I did not wake him when he fell asleep.

6

I was seven years old at the time. In the middle of that night, while I was still sleeping, Miruna awoke and got out of bed, and without anyone hearing, wearing only her nightshirt with the pattern of blue flowers, she went out of the room onto the porch, where the darkness was bottomless. She was not afraid. She walked barefoot over the grass in the yard to the bench by the gate, the one sheltered by the apple tree that numbered each autumn. She was alone in the darkness, oblivious to the cold, following a murmur, as if something were calling her, summoning her to a meeting, as she told me later. And then she heard from on high a body borne through the air on rustling wings, agile and strong. It stood ten paces away from her, incarnate as a tall youth, with the face of Constantine Berca as a young man, from the time of the Battle of Rahova, with wings of dazzling white that were able to slice through the heavens in flight but a hinderance when he walked on the earth. At his waist he wore a sword with an ivory handle, chased with gold and embedded with precious stones. Visible on the hilt was the only seal Miruna had learned to recognize, because she had seen it on the cover of one of Grandfather's books: it was the symbol of the Angel of the Story. It was he. She recognized him right away. Miruna understood she'd been called to meet one of the emperors of this world, the one who had watched over our closeness to Grandfather, and showing no fear of such a creature of vapor and smoke, she inquired:

"Who is troubling Grandpa's sleep?"

He left the question unanswered, though he did tell her other things. From the Angel of the Story Miruna found out that Niculae Berca remembered each tale specially for us, that each joke and each smile concealed something, a memory that was not always necessarily happy, a string of births and deaths, a string of events that were transformed for our eyes into matter just right for the tale. He had taught Grandfather the tale of the Gentle Ones and of the last unicorn, slain by sadness, the tale of the fabulous beasts with their fantastical shapes, which men had at times encountered in the Făgăraș Mountains, and all the other tales whose only purpose was to illuminate for children their golden age. But the two of them did not talk for long since the rustle of a dusky wing was heard from the upper air, the Angel of Death, with eyes like glowing coals in a beautiful face, the Empress of Silence. Her weapon was a diamond sword that cast rays of darkness which could quench even the brightness of the full moon and the stars. On seeing her, the Angel of the Story drew his double-edged sword and rushed up into the heavens, transforming himself into a fearsome warrior. He shouted to the Angel of Death in an unknown tongue, and Miruna thought she understood it as a threat, an ultimatum, that he would vanquish her and banish her from Evil Vale forever because that village was now under his dominion and tutelage, from Our Lady's Crag to the foot of Mount Nehoiu, far into the mountain wilderness, that no one would ever die there again and everything would be frozen as if in amber. But the Angel of Silence did not flinch. Their clash thundered above the clouds. At each blow, the cart pole of the Big Dipper sank nearer to Earth, until it was touching the summit of the Knoll, and then it bent and sprang back into the firmament. So violent was the clash the sky buckled beneath their feet. During the battle, Miruna saw reflected in the water at the edge of the old well an image as if from afar, a village over which a dying wind blew its deathly gust. There were no more stories, no more legends of old women who lived for more than a hundred years and knew how to cast spells with grains of wheat, there was nothing, nothing of the village that in days gone by had seemed destined to live for-ever. Then Miruna looked up once more into the firmament and saw them no longer, for they had flown still locked in combat deep into the upper air. And the battle was so fierce that Miruna under-stood that Grandfather himself was at stake. The end of the battle was like a dream for her. The Angel of the Story returned alone from the heights, triumphant, although we know today that battles between angels have no clear-cut outcomes, no logical consistency. It was not as Miruna had understood it — when it is a question of angels, things are never as we understand them. A summit loomed that looked like the edge of an abyss, a long slope covered in slip-pery grass, at the end of which stretched a wide plain, a boundless expanse of sorrow. If you reached out to it, your arms met noth-ingness and boundlessness at the same time, as in the extinction of death, it is said, the soul returns to the body and thanks it for its succor and kisses it from head to toe in an embrace of spirit and passion that will be the last. Beyond the bourn, Grandfather will be allowed to return from the world of the Angel of Silence from time to time because Miruna will miss him. The portals will be opened, and Miruna will be able to meet him again, and they will sit talking at midnight. He will be able to see nothing but her eyes, as if he were gazing through a very narrow window. He will see the same eyes as in the time of the first stories, and each time he will promise Miruna:

"Know that I shall come again."

After that short moment, time's spindle began to turn, and the Angel of Silence flew over the village one hundred times more, then and at other times, and there was no one to ward her off or to cast stones into her fine net, and that spindle turned swiftly back to the present, the present of Miruna's golden age, and she saw the aftermath of the battle of the angels floating skyward like wisps of smoke. Then the murmur fell silent in the far-off reaches, and she saw nothing more.

The next morning, Miruna awoke in great terror. Dreams had harried her the whole night, and later she told me all, just as I have told it to you now. It had been a night like no other. Miruna heard the white cockerel somewhere near the house. She saw the rays of the sun falling on the white cloth in the window, placed there to keep the light from disturbing our sleep. Miruna went out of the room, the same way as in her dream, and when she reached the porch she heard the sound of weeping. It might have been Mother, maybe it was Grandmother. Miruna did not weep, because at first she understood nothing. She was merely frightened. But as soon as she entered Grandfather's room, she saw that everything was changed, that no angel could ever lift his eyelids now. She went up to him and stroked his cheek. Miruna saw at that age the visage of death and its purpose, which was to separate the two halves of any love with a wall of clay. On the night of Grandfather's passing, Miruna had a nightmare in which she saw a battle in the sky above our yard. And when she awoke at dawn, with the heavy feeling that everything had been real, she saw. She did not cry at first. She went up to him. She stroked his hand and sensed he was far away and strange. Then she suddenly thought herself cursed to remain in a dark place with no exit, a place that bordered on no other place, a place that opened onto nothingness. Grandfather had left, abandoning her there. And it was the first morning without him in Evil Vale, in the chill of a world in which nothing could be as before. It's not fair, thought Miruna, in my dream it was different, our angel was victorious, Grandpa was supposed to stay here, to continue the story. Only yesterday he told us the story of how Oarță Aman returned from the world of shadows to do battle with Colonel von Ziese. Why did it finish like this? By way of an answer, grandfather's face, now so pale, bore the seal of the only thing that cannot be turned back. The wrinkles had stretched out, and Miruna no longer knew this face, livid and motionless, since it resembled that youth of long ago who had been called by the same name and whom she had seen only in photographs yellowed with age. And there the golden age of our life came to an end, with whose passing we could no longer be beguiled or deceived by anything, not by shadows, tales, illusions, or promises. That morning was our banishment from paradise, the estrangement. It was then that the real world began, that we took our first steps on the earth. It hurt that Grandfather had left this world while he still owed us an endless string of stories. They remained unfinished because we were born too late or because he had died too soon, the same as happens with many encounters in this world, encounters that are never complete, never consummated.

It was the first time either Miruna or I had seen the face of a corpse. She sat motionless on the edge of the bed, gazing at the lifeless face. It was an empty face, devoid of smiles, hidden and distant, a face whose eyes had once had the same color as hers. Grandfather had told her the tale of the whole world as if it were a game, as if an enchantment, a game that perhaps makes no sense to anyone else, but was to remain alive in Miruna as much as in me, somewhere near the miraculous ends of the earth, which lie unexpectedly close, buried under this hill, for if the tale were not true, I wouldn't have told it to you.

1992–2007

AUTHOR'S AFTERWORD

I read J.R.R. Tolkien's *The Hobbit* in Romanian translation when I was ten, having found the book by accident in a bookstore. I was living with my parents then in a small town on the Danubian Plain, where nobody knew much of anything about hobbits. The town had a small bookstore not much larger than our living room. Tolkien's book was not the usual choice for a Romanian reader of my age, and its translation into Romanian was something new in the 1970s. I was intrigued at first: what sort of creature is a hobbit? Are they dwarves? Are they a different sort of human, smaller? Today I know it was just the wonderful construction of an inspired storyteller based on a theme borrowed from Nordic mythology. I was fascinated by the story and read it with a mixture of awe and surprise. To my disappointment, no other authors were discussing hobbits at all. When I moved to America many years later, I discovered that the word *hobbit* comes from two Old Saxon words, *hol* and *bytla*, and when combined they yield the equivalent of *hole-builder*. These kinds of details are important because they have much to say about an imaginary world born in a society that still retained traces in its legends of a time long past. I find it particularly important that Tolkien developed such elements rooted in traditional culture.

I used to spend my summer and winter vacations at my grandmother's country house in the Carpathians. Called Nucşoara, the village lies in a valley surrounded by the white peaks of mountains. My grandmother's domain was a completely different world. It was the last remnant of the old traditional environment of peasants, a world that today no longer exists but whose landscape surfaces every so often in some breathtaking *National Geographic* photo spread. Back in the 1970s, I had the chance to meet the old-timers who fought in WW II and listen to them tell their stories. Some of them had never attended school and did not know how to read or write, but could nevertheless remember interesting episodes from real life and relate them with consummate passion and skill. I had the opportunity to know shepherds who lived the life of hermits and, in their mountain isolation, would not talk to another human for days. I spoke with people who would not go to town for years on end and were genuinely convinced that any encroachment by modernity meant a loss of quality of life. It was a society very different from the one I witnessed during the school months, when I would go back to my parents and live a modern urban life, going to school and visiting bookstores.

This was my firsthand experience with traditional Balkan society. I heard the stories as a child, and later I compared what I remembered with other accounts from various sources. Perhaps the moment when I understood what I had witnessed as a child was at the beginning of the 1990s when I read Mircea Eliade's *Le mythe de l'éternel retour*. This was about an anthropological study conducted by Constantin Brăiloiu in northern Transylvania during the interwar period. Brăiloiu was interested in studying the various collected versions of a folk ballad about a fay of the mountains who fell in love with a shepherd. Because the shepherd was betrothed to a girl from the village, the fay killed him out of jealousy by pushing him off a cliff. That was the way it went in the ballad. After a detailed investigation and comparing the various versions of the ballad from different villages, Brăiloiu zoomed in on a particular village as the potential source of the original version. He discovered by interviewing the village inhabitants that the core of the ballad was based on a real event, something that had actually happened a few decades earlier. In fact, he was able to identify an old lady whose groom had died many years ago just one day before their wedding was to take place. Enough elements corresponded to believe that this personal tragedy was the very genesis of the ballad. Of course, no supernatural power was involved to push the man off the cliff: the actual death was different, but the human tragedy was the same. This was the episode that Brăiloiu discovered, and when I read about it in Eliade's book, the idea had a profound impact on me as it was exactly what I had seen with my own eyes.

Over the course of centuries, historical facts tend to become transformed into either rumors or ballads or legends. Such an example is the building of Argeș Monastery. Completed around 1517, it was turned into a ballad with legendary characters in the 19th century, which in turn found its way into our school textbooks in the chapter on old literature, and with pretty much the same reverence that the Finns have for their *Kalevala*.

I remember a legend I heard in Nucșoara about the origin of the only dissolution lake in Romania (sinkholes might be rather common in Florida or in the former Yugoslavia, but are very rare in the Carpathians). This lake happened to be found in the same village of my maternal grandparents where I used to spend my summers. The real-life event took place in the 19th century, and the legend about a curse causing the sinking of a garden was a later invention. I heard someone tell it, and now I'm at a loss to explain how someone could invent such a thing. By the time they were told to me, a great many historical events had already become clouded and were well on their natural path of transforming into full-blown legend: the War of Independence against the Ottoman Empire (1877–78); the participation of the village men in those battles; the brief episode of German military units occupying Romania in 1917; the anti-communist guerrilla resistance (1949–58) — all of these were actual historical events whereas the future was concealed by a veil of uncertainty and memory struggled against trauma.

The fact that in my childhood I was able to witness on numerous occasions the process whereby real facts are transformed into the rudiments of ballads or the seeds of legends was possible largely to an accident of the local history. Communist agricultural policies wiped out whole villages and traditional society in Romania with them. Romanian villages were "modernized," and this happened mostly in the 1950s, so by the time I was growing up in the 1970s and '80s the damage had been done. Yet the geographical region where my grandparents lived was of little economic value to the communist vision of agriculture. In most of the rest of Romania, farming land was combined into collective farming enterprises that did no one any good. The Communists, however, could not implement this policy in the mountain villages — the houses were too sporadic and there were no decent roads and no infrastructure to consolidate into a single large collective farm for several hundred families. So these isolated hamlets were left alone for some decades, a few corners on the map untouched by the communist regime, the last outposts of traditional society. I witnessed the final days of that archaic world. The old folks passed away, and their children scattered to the four corners of the world in search of a better life.

I left Romania in 1996. I completed Miruna's story in California.

Bogdan Suceavă
Irvine, September 2013

NOTES

p. 10   *Pitești*: an important commercial and industrial center located on the Argeș River; the capital of Argeș County and its largest city.

p. 13   *King Carol*: Carol I (1839–1914) born Prince Karl of Hohenzollern -Sigmaringen, elected Domnitor (ruler) of the Romanian United Principalities on April 20, 1866, upon the ouster of Alexandru Ioan Cuza (see below). He declared Romania a sovereign nation in 1877 and then led the Romanian Army to victory against the Ottoman Empire in the Russo-Turkish War. He was crowned King of Romania on March 26, 1881.

p. 13   *Prâslea the Brave*: hero of the Romanian folk tale "Prâslea the Brave and the Golden Apples."

p. 13   *Stephen the Great*: Stephen III of Moldavia (1433–1504); as Voivode (Prince) of Moldavia (1457–1504) he was victorious in 46 of 48 battles against the Ottoman Empire as well as winning battles against Polish and Hungarian armies.

p. 13   *the brave Greuceanu*: hero in Romanian folklore who sets the Sun and Moon free after finding they've been stolen.

p. 13   *Anton Pann*: (1790–1854), Romanian poet who wrote the volume *A Collection of Proverbs, or the Story of the Word*.

p. 13   *May-the-Bells-Slay-Him*: a representation of the devil in Romanian folklore.

p. 15   The Spark: the Romanian daily *Scînteia* that was the official organ of the Communist Party of Romania from the 1950s to 1989.

p. 16   *Făgăraș Mountains*: highest mountain range of the southern Carpathians.

p. 17   *war in Bulgaria*: Romanian War of Independence (note below).

p. 17   *Muscel Regiment*: from Câmpulung Muscel and surrounding area.

p. 21   *Battle of Rahova*: during the Russo-Turkish War, the important Bulgarian port city of Oryahovo on the Danube was liberated by Romanian forces after a three-day battle in November 1877.

p. 21   *Romanian War of Independence*: or Russo-Turkish War, 1877–78. The Romanians were allied with the Russian Empire in defeating the Ottoman Turks.

p. 21   *Argeș Monastery*: Eastern Orthodox monastery located in Curtea de Argeș and built between 1512 and 1517 under the rule of Voivode Neagoe Basarab (ruled 1512–21).

p. 23   *Câmpulung*: or Câmpulung Muscel in full, city in Argeș County, oldest city in Wallachia and its first capital.

p. 24   *Domnești*: a commune (of villages) in Argeș County.

p. 26   *in Prince Cuza's time*: Alexandru Ioan Cuza, or Alexandru Ioan I, (1820–73) was Voivode of Moldavia, Voivode of Wallachia, and later Domnitor of the Romanian United Principalities. In his youth he was a leading figure of the Revolution of 1848 in Moldavia.

p. 31   *Our Lady's River*: (Râul Doamnei) originating in the Carpathians, a tributary to the Argeș just north of Pitești.

p. 34   *Michael the Brave*: (1558–1601), as Voivode of Wallachia, Transylvania, and Moldavia he represented the first time all three principalities were united under a single ruler.

p. 35   *the battlefields of Plevna and Vidin*: Pleven is a city in northern Bulgaria that was an Ottoman garrison to block the advance of the joint Russian and Romanian forces during the Russo-Turkish War. The Siege of Plevna took place over the latter half of 1877, and four battles were fought before the Ottoman forces surrendered. Vidin is a port town on the Danube in northwestern Bulgaria. The battle took place between January 14 and February 4, 1878, with the Romanian Army eliminating the last important Ottoman fortress on the river.

p. 38 *Prince Ghika*: Grigore IV, Voivode of Wallachia 1822–28, the first Romanian to reign in Wallachia after the Phanariote period (1716–1821) when the Ottoman sultan appointed Greek princes to rule there.

p. 43 *Nehoiu*: sometimes written as Negoiu, at 2,535 meters the second highest mountain in the Romanian Carpathians.

p. 44 *Rock Breaker*: a character from folklore.

p. 48 *Master Builder Manole*: in a Romanian folk ballad published by Vasile Alecsandri in 1852, Manole is the mythical chief architect of the Curtea de Argeș Monastery in Wallachia.

p. 50 *Pasărea Monastery*: located near Bucharest, founded in 1813.

p. 54 *Săliște and Mărginime*: villages in southern Transylvania, the region from which some of the families in the story come.

p. 61 *Vlăsiei Forest*: Codrii Vlăsiei, a forest that once covered parts of southern Romania.

p. 62 *the Știrbey line*: a noble family in Romania (see note below).

p. 62 *Topolog Valley*: formed of a tributary to the Olt River that passes through Argeș and Vâlcea counties.

p. 64 *Vlașca County*: A defunct county in southern Muntenia.

p. 68 *"Unaging Youth and Deathless Life"*: a fantasy tale published in 1872 in *Romanian Legends and Tales* by Petre Ispirescu (1830–87).

p. 68 *Ileana Cosânzeana*: in Romanian folklore, the most beautiful of the fays, the personification of feminine beauty.

p. 75 *the oka*: an old unit of volume roughly equal to one quart.

p. 75 *Matei Basarab*: (1588–1654), Voivode of Wallachia 1632–54.

p. 76 *Prince Ştirbey*: Barbu Dimitrie Ştirbey (1799–1869), last Voivode of Wallachia (1848–53 and 1854–56) before the province's political union with Moldova, which after 1859 yielded the state of Romania.

p. 82 *Constanţa*: formerly known as Tomis, the oldest city in Romania, located on the Black Sea coast near the border with Bulgaria.

p. 91 *"A church of stone"*: a reference to the Corbii de Piatră Monastery, founded in the 14th century in Corbi, Argeş County, and reestablished in 1512 under the reign of Neagoe Basarab.

p. 91 *Învârtita Lake*: formed by a sinkhole in Nucşoara in Argeş County.

p. 96 *not the scorpion or the woodpecker*: fantasy characters of feminine gender in Ispirescu's "Unaging Youth and Deathless Life" (see note above).

p. 100 *Our Lady of the Rocks*: local legend had it that during the Mongol invasions a princess of Wallachia took shelter in the deep forests of the valley. The village of Domneşti and the Râul Doamnei (Our Lady's River) take their names from this legend.

p. 100 *Aleodorus the Emperor*: tale by Petre Ispirescu.

p. 102 *the feast of Ss. Constantine and Elena*: traditionally celebrated on May 21 according to the Romanian Orthodox calendar, it marks the transhumance date when the herds move from the valley to the mountains for summer grazing.

p. 102 *Plain of Teleorman*: part of the Danubian Plain in central Wallachia.

p. 106 *Vale of Tears*: a magic place in Ispirescu's "Unaging Youth and Deathless Life"; whoever stepped in the vale would be overcome by a longing for childhood and his birthplace and would feel the urge to return even if the place no longer existed.

p. 110 *Ion Creangă's story "White Arab"*: also known as "The Story of Harap Alb," a Romanian fantasy tale written in 1877.

p. 110 *in three different wars*: Russo-Turkish War (Rahova); World War I (Turtucaia); World War II (Odessa).

p. 110 *Saint Filofteia*: an Eastern Orthodox saint, born in the 13th century near Tarnovo, Bulgaria, whose relics have been kept since the end of the 14th century in the Curtea de Argeș Monastery. Her cult is particularly powerful in traditional Romanian culture.

p. 110 *crossing of the Danube in 1877*: when the Romanian Army joined up with the Russian Army to fight the Ottomans in the Russo-Turkish War.

p. 110 *reunification celebrations of 1918*: the union of Transylvania with Romania was declared on December 1, 1918.

p. 113 *Muntenia*: historical province of Romania known as Greater Wallachia.

p. 118 *Battle of Posada*: November 1330, Wallachia under Basarab I defeated the army of the Kingdom of Hungary led by King Charles Robert de Anjou (1288–1342).

p. 118 *Nicolae Iorga*: (1871–1940) Romanian historian, politician, poet, and writer, murdered in 1940 by an Iron Guard assassination squad.

p. 118 *Basarab the Great*: Basarab I (1310–52), founder of first Romanian ruling dynasty.

p. 120 *dynasty of Cuman princes*: the dynasty founded by Basarab I was of Cuman origin.

p. 120 Prolem sine matre creatam: a child born without a mother.

p. 120 *State Security troops*: after 1949, an anticommunist guerrilla movement operated in the Făgăraș Mountains, going by the name "Hajduks of the Muscel." Never numbering more than twenty men, the band was captured on May 20, 1958 and sixteen of its members executed. Other groups in other parts of the Carpathians also resisted the communist regime that was installed by the Soviet Union in the aftermath of World War Two.

p. 121 *Râmeț Monastery*: located in Alba Country, Transylvania, dating to the 13th century.

ABOUT THE AUTHOR

Bogdan Suceavă was born in Curtea de Argeş, Romania, in 1969. He attended university in Bucharest and then came to the United States to pursue graduate studies, ultimately receiving his Ph.D. in Mathematics from Michigan State University. An author of five novels and two collections of short stories, his work has appeared in English in numerous journals — such as *Absinthe: New European Writing*, *Red Mountain Review*, *Review of Contemporary Fiction*, and *Two Lines* — and in anthologies. His novel *Coming from an Off-Key Time*, in Alistair Ian Blyth's translation, was published by Northwestern University Press in 2011. Suceavă is currently Professor of Mathematics at California State University, Fullerton.

ABOUT THE TRANSLATOR

A native of Sunderland, England, Alistair Ian Blyth has resided for many years in Bucharest. His many translations from Romanian include *Little Fingers* by Filip Florian, *Our Circus Presents* by Lucian Dan Teodorovici, *Occurrence in the Immediate Unreality* by Max Blecher, and *Coming from an Off-Key Time* by Bogdan Suceavă.

Miruna, a Tale by Bogdan Suceavă
is translated by Alistair Ian Blyth from the original
Romanian *Miruna, o poveste*, published by Curtea Veche
Publishing in Bucharest in 2007.

Cover by Dan Mayer
Flyleaf image by Kaatya Kelly
Frontispiece photograph from the author's archives
Design by Silk Mountain Ltd.
Typeset in Janson Pro, titles in Futura

FIRST EDITION

Published in 2014 by
Twisted Spoon Press
P.O. Box 21 – Preslova 12
150 21 Prague 5
Czech Republic
www.twistedspoon.com

Printed and bound in the Czech Republic by PB Tisk

Distributed to the trade by
CENTRAL BOOKS
99 Wallis Road
London, E9 5LN
United Kingdom
www.centralbooks.com

SCB DISTRIBUTORS
15608 South New Century Drive
Gardena, CA 90248-2129
USA
www.scbdistributors.com